MARY WICKIZER BURGESS

THE RELUCTANT WITNESS

Complete and Unabridged

LINFORD
Leicester

First published in Great Britain

First Linford Edition
published 2017

A catalogue record for this book is available
from the British Library.

ISBN 978–1–4448–3490–1

Published by
F. A. Thorpe (Publishing)
Anstey, Leicestershire

Set by Words & Graphics Ltd.
Anstey, Leicestershire
Printed and bound in Great Britain by
T. J. International Ltd., Padstow, Cornwall

This book is printed on acid-free paper

THE RELUCTANT WITNESS

Attorney Gail Brevard is faced with a big problem when her key witness, Clinton Bolt, goes on the lam to Mexico. An arson death and an unexpected kidnapping are just a few of the issues she and her colleagues must deal with while preparing for a trial with millions of dollars at stake. A whirlwind trip across the border gives Gail the upper hand — but not for long, as the criminals are still at large. Where will the unknown assailant strike next — and who will be the next victim?

Books by *Mary Wickizer Burgess*
in the *Linford Mystery Library:*

THE PURPLE GLOVE MURDERS
HANGOVER HILL
THE MISSING ATTORNEY

with *Ana R. Morlan*
GRAVE WATERS

1

'Excuse me . . . '

The woman leaning on the counter scribbled on the margins of the work sheet in front of her with a stubby pencil. She paused, lifted her shoulders and looked up in the direction of the disembodied voice. Tired eyes took in the stranger standing in front of her.

He had been tall once, but his back was bent, as if he had spent a lifetime hunched over something. A desk maybe . . . or, more likely, a bar. He wore a white T-shirt tucked into faded blue jeans. His tweed sports jacket had been expensive, but now looked frayed around the cuffs. He had one piece of scuffed leather-trimmed luggage — Skyway, she judged, from the '50s.

'Yes, can I help you?' She pushed a stray wisp of hair back from her sweaty forehead.

'I'd like to purchase a ticket, one way, to San Miguel.'

She could tell from the way he pronounced 'San Miguel' that he was probably Spanish-speaking, although he looked *gringo*. His hair, pulled back in a scraggly ponytail, was too black. He had dyed it, but hadn't bothered to touch up the day-old whiskers that had been blond at one time but were now gray.

'You want to take a bus all the way to S.M.? Most folks fly into Mexico City or León and take the bus from there. It's a long bumpy ride with quite a few stopovers. It'll take you hours longer that way.'

'That's all right.' He smiled at her, and her heart skipped a little beat. He had the bluest eyes she'd ever seen. He wasn't handsome, but there was a subtle charisma about him all the same. 'I've got all the time in the world.'

'Well, let me see what's available. You know these lines don't run by a regular schedule. It's hit or miss.' She pulled out a well-worn binder and began leafing through, jotting notes down on a piece of paper with the chewed-off pencil, chatting as she went. 'I can get you on the next bus out of here, but there'll be a few side stops. You should get into León about midnight and layover there. Then reach S.M. about noon tomorrow. If you want a faster ride, you'll have to wait until tomorrow morning here . . . there's a boarding house down the street. Either way, you can't get there until tomorrow earliest. Now, if you flew, I could have you there late this evening — '

'No, let's go with the first bus. I'd just as soon be on my way. I don't care about the layover. *¿Cuánto?* How much?'

His easy lapse into Spanish convinced her he was fluent. Not a puzzle. He was either an expat returning to his base of operations, or someone used to going back and forth across the border. Maybe on the lam? Wouldn't be surprising.

'Eighty US bucks for the ride to León . . . another fifty to take you on in to S.M.' She paused to see how he took that.

'All right,' he drawled, pulling a large rolled-up wad of cash out of his inside jacket pocket. He peeled off six twenties and a ten. 'Will that do it?'

She counted them back at him. 'Yep, that's fine.'

The bills felt new and crisp in her hand. She hoped they weren't phony. 'Now,' she continued, 'you know they will want to see your papers at each stop?'

He nodded.

'It's better if you let me record your documents here, your passport and good ID. I'll give you an FMM, a Tourist Permit Form that states you passed through customs here all right, and that'll make it easier for you later on. You won't be able to get back into the States without it, but it's good for 180 days. You've got your passport, don't you?'

'Sure.' He reached into the other breast pocket and pulled out a worn leatherette case. In one side was the thin little passport book and in the other was a brand-new Texas-issued driver's license. The photos in each were similar, and looked as though they had been taken yesterday, except, of course, for the straggly pale hairs on his chin. Same darkened hair, same intense eyes. No charming smile, but an interesting face all the same.

She hesitated a moment as she studied the photos. 'That's an unusual name,' she said. 'Kind of old-fashioned. Named after someone in your family?'

'No.'

He didn't offer anything further on the topic of his name, and she didn't bother to pursue it. She had been right the first time. He was probably on the lam. Oh well, not hers to wonder why. 'All right,' she said. 'I'll get your paperwork documented and your tickets issued.'

She busied herself for several minutes, filling in the standard form for the customs people, and pulling the two bus tickets. 'Here,' she said finally, shoving them across the counter.

Their fingers touched as he reached for the paperwork, and she felt electricity pass between them that took her breath away. Flustered, she turned back to the ticket log for a moment to regain her bearings. *What an idiot I am*, she mused. *He's a loser, for sure. And I don't have the time or energy to even think about what might or might not be.*

'Have a good trip . . . ' she began as she looked back up. But she only caught the outer door swinging shut out of the corner of her eye.

And just like that, he was gone.

2

'Gone? How could he be gone?' Gail Brevard tried to still the icy chill that had started down her spine as soon as her associate in Arizona, Charles Walton, had given her the news.

'Where could he be? I thought the U.S. Marshals had agreed to keep an eye on him?'

'Not 24/7, Gail. They weren't going to do that. I thought he was fine. I was trying to keep tabs on him myself. And I did talk to the managers at the ranch. They seemed to think he was doing all right. Had dried out pretty easily, and seemed content to be there. What can I say? I had no idea he was planning this.'

'Do you have any idea at all how long he's been out of touch? Or where he might have gone? Maybe there's a woman involved. Maybe he just took off on his own for a bit. Some people can't handle being watched like that.' She paused a moment. 'He's pretty much a loner, I think. Probably got to him and he flipped.' She didn't want to even begin to think of the other possibility — that the people their charge was scheduled to testify against had gotten wind of it and had taken steps to ensure he would never make it back to the already-scheduled trial.

She made a quick decision. 'All right. Let me bring Hugo in and see if there's any possibility he or one of his operatives can get out there and try and pick up the trail. Can you put him up, or should I get him a room there?'

'No, of course I'll be glad to put him up. It'll be good to see him.'

Charles and Hugo Goldthwaite, Gail's go-to P.I.s, were the best of friends. They had weathered many a storm together, and Charles looked forward to the visit, although not under these circumstances, of course.

'Gail,' he added, 'I'm so very sorry about the screw-up. I know it throws a monkey wrench into the trial. But honestly, I had no idea he was going to do this. He really did a number on me.'

'Don't worry about it. We'll figure something out. I'll get back to you as soon as I know if Hugo can get out there.'

'Okay. I'll wait for your call.'

The phone clicked, and Gail sat there for a moment pondering this new turn of events. Just when things seemed to be going fine, something always came along to upset the apple cart.

She texted Hugo and her partner, Conrad 'Connie' Osterlitz, asking them to join her as soon as they could get free. She thought Connie had a court appearance that morning, but with any luck it hadn't taken long and he would be back in the office shortly.

She pushed back from her desk and walked over to the big window looking out over Cathcart's bustling Main Street. The Court House, known locally as the Hall of Justice, was in one direction, the town house she and Connie shared in the other. Further on, in the upscale development known as Long Hills, was her childhood home, where her mother, Alberta Norris, and Erle, her brother with special needs, resided.

These three compass points made up the nexus of her existence. All of her hopes and dreams, and most of the people she truly cared about, were contained within that tiny triangulation. But Main Street, between the law offices of Brevard and Osterlitz and the Hall of Justice — that was her baseline.

In the midst of her musings came a quick rap on the door, and Hugo Goldthwaite entered with a question on his face. 'What's up, boss?' he said. 'Got your text and I guess it means what I think.'

'Hope I didn't take you away from anything important,' she said. 'It's pretty bad. I just got a call from Charles and it looks like our chickie flew the coop. Bolt's gone, and Charles has no idea where . . . or why.'

'I had a bad feeling about that guy from the beginning. What's the plan? Are you going to tell Ralph?'

Gail hesitated. Clinton Bolt, their missing witness, was a material piece in the upcoming Del Monaco trial. The patriarch of the family, Antonio 'Nino' Del Monaco, had died earlier in the year at the ripe old age of 94. Gail and Connie had assisted the old man in constructing his last will and testament, a complex document that established an irrevocable trust benefiting Nino's youngest grandson, Ralph.

Contrary to their advice, Nino refused to list any of his other possible heirs — Ralph's two uncles, an aunt and various cousins — even in a nominal manner, thus leaving the document open to litigation. And just as Gail and Connie predicted, once the old man was safely buried, his descendants banded together and brought suit to overturn the trust, claiming Ralph had engaged in undue influence upon his grandfather, thus successfully alienating him from the other rightful heirs to the Del Monaco fortune.

'Yes. I don't see how we can keep it from him. Hugo, I hate to ask you this, but could you clear your schedule enough to go out there, take a look around, and see if you can figure out just what happened to Bolt? I hate to say it, but there's always the possibility he met with foul play, or was removed from the area against his wishes. But until we know for certain that he just did a runner, I don't want to jump to any conclusions.'

'Right, I'll get on it. I think I can clear some time. I might take one of my guys with me, just for backup. No telling what we might run into there.'

'Charles offered to put you up. We'll need to let him know your plans as soon as possible.'

'Got it. I'll get back to you in a bit.'

After he left, Gail sat back at her desk. She didn't need to consult her messy little paper calendar propped between the keyboard and the monitor to confirm that the all-important Del Monaco trial was scheduled for August 21st. The July 4th holiday weekend had just ended, so they had about six weeks to get this situation back under control.

She would need to change things up, to put another defense plan in motion, just in case Clint Bolt had bolted for good.

3

Clint Bolt heaved a sigh of relief when his taxi came to a shuddering stop on the narrow cobblestone street in front of a bright blue wooden door set solidly into a terracotta wall.

He suspected he was getting too old for all these shenanigans. The physical demands on him made keeping his mental acuity a challenge. He couldn't afford any slip-ups this time. Everything depended on him staying one step ahead of everyone, including Ralph Del Monaco's defense team, no matter how good their intentions were.

He climbed out of the cab, collected his battered bag and paid the driver. He had been able to exchange some of his US dollars for pesos at the layover in León the night before. He was careful to tip, but not too generously. No need for anyone to think he had extra cash on him.

Once the driver had clattered away

down the cobbled road, he stood there for a moment, as if taking in the quaint scenery and breathing in the crisp air fresh off the nearby mountains. Certain at last that he wasn't being watched, he bent quickly, lifted a decorative pot set into the concrete walkway next to the door, and retrieved a single key which he fit into the double deadbolts, turned it back and forth to clear the locks, and pushed open the rustic blue door.

Once inside, he just as rapidly shut and locked the door behind him, taking the extra precaution of shoving a security bar across the entrance to further discourage trespassers. Bag in hand, he made his way through the cool, dim entry and on into the jewel of a courtyard beyond.

He paused to take in and relish the sight he had been longing for. Each time he returned here, the still beauty of the tiny brick-floored patio, open to the blue sky above, enchanted him and calmed his soul. A lemon tree, bending from the weight of ripe yellow fruit and already fragrant with the pinkish blossoms of the next cycle, caught a few slanting rays of late-afternoon sun. Opposite in a shaded corner, a tall avocado tree, dark green leaves still glistening with moisture, promised nourishment within arm's reach. A few rough-hewn wooden chairs and tables faced toward a tinkling stone fountain in the very center of this private paradise.

Bolt didn't stop here, as much as he was tempted, but moved on to a pair of solid double doors on the opposite side of the garden. The same key worked here also and again, once he was safely inside the *casa* proper, he carefully locked and bolted the doors behind him.

He was under no illusions. Anyone could break in to any place at any time. But at least he had taken all the precautions possible.

Only when he was safely inside the tiny adobe-walled room did he carefully set down his suitcase and head to a mission-style chair in front of a small functional chimenea set into the whitewashed wall, the only source of heat in the *casita*.

Finally, he collapsed and let the relief

wash over him. He sighed in contentment. This had been the best decision he had ever made in his whole messed-up life.

Some years ago, when he was still capable of making good money and had put aside a bit of savings, he had purchased this tiny one-room *casita* outright on a whim. In spite of all the bad luck he'd had since, he had held on to it at all costs. This was his ace in the hole, his very own 'safe' house. He had purchased the property under yet another phony name, and not many people in his life knew about it. There were Miguel and Luci Hernández, of course, the local couple who kept tabs on the place for him. And one or two others, long-time friends, who would not betray him . . . he hoped. Other than those few calculated risks, it was the perfect hideaway. And if there was anything he needed in the world right now, it was a place to hide.

'Clinton Bolt' wasn't his birth name, either. He had made it up when he first went on the road. He had always liked the actor, Clint Eastwood, mainly for his laconic voice and silent self-assuredness. He thought he resembled the performer in some ways — and Eastwood also played piano, which made it something of a no-brainer. He had imagined people calling him 'Clint' and making the connection between the two of them. Ironically, however, most people called him 'Bolt' instead, which had been something of a letdown.

At the same time he purchased the property, he had used the rest of his money to set up an account at the local Banco de Mexico that paid a small monthly stipend to the Hernández couple, and also kept up minimum payments on the utilities. There was enough of a balance there, he had calculated, to keep the concern going for as long as he was likely to need it. He'd established paperwork to pass the deed on to the Hernández family whenever he cashed in his chips.

He got up and peered into a small ancient refrigerator chugging away in the brightly tiled kitchen nook in one corner of the room. Yes, Luci had stocked it with a few staples, enough to keep him going for several days. He had gotten a message to them just before he left Phoenix, a stupid touristy postcard with one word on it, '*Hoy*,' the code word he had established with them at the outset of this venture.

He was lucky, he knew. Miguel and Luci were loyal to him. But then, the demands he made on them weren't great. He only asked that they check on the place from time to time, just to be sure no squatters or vandals crept in, and to keep up the maintenance. He would let them know, through the code word, when he had need of it. They had agreed without question or conditions, and he was certain the monthly payment in their favor had secured the deal. It meant they would always have food on the table, no matter how their fortunes played out in other matters.

The only other furniture in the single room included a small pine table and two primitive straight chairs, a single cot with a colorful *serape* draped over it on one wall and, incongruously, an old upright piano on the other.

He went to the piano, sat down gingerly on the hard bench, and reached out and shoved back the keyboard cover. He stared down at the yellowish ivory and dull black keys. Several of them were chipped. He suspected the instrument was out of tune.

He placed his left hand, fingers splayed, over the bass end of the keyboard and executed a few stride moves, walking the chords up and down. He stretched out his right hand and did a few ascending and descending runs from memory, trying to harmonize the fills with 10th combinations on his left, and humming a bit of 'St. James Infirmary', his go-to piece.

He stopped in the midst of a run. The arthritis in his knuckles would not allow them to bend properly. And it had been too long. He could no longer remember the notes, which always before had come at his bidding. The music did not flow from him easily as it had for so many years . . . so many years ago.

Angrily, he slammed the cover back down over the keys, hard. His watering eyes travelled to one of the upper cupboards. Was it still there?

A few minutes later he was seated at the bleached kitchen table. Shaking, he carefully poured a few ounces of Guanojuato tequila into one of Luci's plain water glasses. He downed it neat and sat back to let the warm glow overtake him.

He couldn't get out of his mind an old saying his preacher father had repeated often: *The road to hell is paved with good intentions.*

He hoped he would be able to sleep tonight, in this paradise of his own making.

4

'But where in the world could he be hiding? And, more importantly, *why*?' Connie had hurried in, straight from his morning session at the Hall of Justice, after receiving Gail's urgent text.

'Charles doesn't have a clue. The last time he checked on Bolt, he was fine, or as fine as he could be under the circumstances. The people at the ranch said he was doing well and had stopped drinking on his own without too much assistance from them. They had tried to get him into some of the group sessions, but he preferred to go it alone.'

'What about the US Marshals? I thought they were going to keep an eye on him?'

'Charles says they sent someone over every few days. But they didn't think he was much of a risk. Of course . . . ' She hesitated, the other possibility floating in the air between them.

'You don't think the Del Monacos got to him?'

'Well, Hugo said it was always a possibility. Bolt didn't think they suspected he had anything on them. But he could have been wrong about that. Also, we don't know anything about Bolt's friends and activities. He could have taken someone else into his confidence; someone who had a different agenda.'

'Right. Well, the sooner Hugo gets out there the better. How's that shaping up?'

'He's got his tickets. Jake's going with him, just in case anything gets out of hand, and he's been in touch with Charles.'

'I don't like this, Gail. The last thing in the world we need is for any of our people to be put in jeopardy out there in Arizona. I don't trust the Del Monaco family any further than I could throw one of them.'

'I know. But I can't think of anything else to do. Can you?'

They sat there silently a moment, each going over all the remote possibilities of 'things that could go wrong' in their minds, trying to come up with some easy solution to a very difficult problem.

Connie thought back to a week ago, when Hugo had approached them about the possibility of using Bolt as a witness. 'It's a long shot, boss,' he had admitted. 'But the guy seems to know what he's talking about. He's looking for a stake and a fresh start, and if what he says is true, Tommy has an awful lot of 'splainin' to do.'

Tommaso 'Tommy' Del Monaco, Nino's oldest son, had expected to inherit the bulk of his father's estate. When he was passed over in favor of his deceased brother's son, Ralph, the titular 'boss' of the family was livid. He had rallied the rest of the family members and filed suit to not only overturn the old man's last will and testament, but he was also demanding compensation from Ralph for putting undue pressure on Nino and taking advantage of his grandfather's frailty in his final days.

Gail and Connie had put together a traditional defense establishing Ralph's *bona fides*, as well as a long list of character witnesses vouching for his credibility, including statements from Nino's doctor and the nursing attendants who had cared for the old man at the end.

An independent accounting firm did a complete appraisal of all the assets of the estate, including the jewels in the crown, the Del Monaco Hotel and Casino enterprises, which included the new concern located on the Nevada side of Lake Tahoe and the older complex in Las Vegas. The rumored Mustang brothel didn't show up, but there was a 'boarding house' located in Storey County that seemed unusually profitable.

All in all, it made for a hefty total. Gail and Connie had talked to Ralph about settling up with Tommy and the others, but he was adamant. 'Papa wanted me to have it all, and I respect his wishes. I'm not going to buckle under to those goons. None of them came to see Papa at the end, when it would have made a big difference to him. He had his reasons for wanting it to go down this way. I think he was tired — and ashamed, really — of all the 'gang' talk. He told me he wanted to be sure everything going forward was going to be legitimate. He wanted me to sell off all the questionable investments and start trying to do some good for a change. The truth is, he got religion at the end of his life, and I want to honor his wishes.'

It had been quite a long speech for Ralph, who normally kept his own counsel. Gail and Connie agreed to move forward with the defense they had cobbled together. But everyone knew it was going to be a difficult task. So when Hugo was contacted by one of his street informants about a possible witness to some of Tommy's underhanded dealings, they agreed to meet Bolt and hear him out.

It wasn't an easy interview. Bolt entered the conference room with Hugo and introductions were made. His clothes were clean, if threadbare, and his grayish-blond hair was slicked back in a short ponytail. The most impressive things about him were his bright blue Paul Newman-like eyes, bloodshot that morning from a heavy bout of drinking the night before. He took a shaky sip of the steaming black coffee Hugo handed him, and waited.

'We understand you are familiar with the Del Monaco family and their operations,' Connie began.

'Yessir. I met Tommy at least 20 years ago, when I was just starting out.'

'Starting out . . . in the entertainment business?'

'Yes. I'm . . . I was a piano player. For a while I had my own trio, and I never had trouble getting gigs . . . jobs. I played Vegas regularly in the early days. Tommy heard me one evening, bought me a couple of drinks, and after that . . . we were friends, I guess.' He took another sip of coffee and sat back, more comfortable now.

'And at some point, he hired you?'

'It was about six months later, I think. During one of our sessions he started talking about this big new hotel they were putting up in at Tahoe. Said he might have a regular job for me there, and would I be interested.'

'And you were.' Connie's comment was

a statement, not a question.

'Yes. I was ready for a change. Going from gig to gig and traveling all over gets tiresome after a while. He said they were willing to pay me on a regular basis — a salary, which is rare in the business. It wasn't a huge amount, but it would be a steady income. If I had some special event or out-of-town show I needed to attend, they said they would be more than willing to give me the leeway for that. Sounded like a pretty good deal to me. So I accepted.'

'How long did you work for the Del Monaco concern in this capacity?'

'Steadily? About five years, I think. But even after I left the salaried position, they always let me come back from time to time, especially if I needed the work. I have no quarrel with them on that account.'

'So why are you here today? Sounds like you had a good deal with them. Why are you willing to testify against them?'

Bolt hesitated before answering. He glanced sideways at Hugo, then took a deep breath.

'To be honest, I've been scared of the Del Monacos ever since that night. I have no idea if they have any notion of what I saw and heard. But I can tell you this — I don't want to test the friendship.'

'But if you testify, you know you *will* be putting yourself in jeopardy,' Gail said. She had kept quiet up until now, but she wanted to be sure Bolt understood and accepted all the implications and possible consequences of his actions.

'Oh sure, I know that. But what I'm hoping is that Ralph will be willing to set me up with enough cash to keep me going for as long as I'm liable to need it. I'm not a young man any longer, and I admit I'm not in the best of health. I could change my name and disappear once the trial is over. I'm prepared to do that, and if Ralph will agree to my terms, I'll be happy to tell you where all the bodies are buried — at least all those I know about.'

Connie raised his eyebrow in that characteristic way he had when things got dicey. He glanced at Gail and she nodded. If Bolt's story was as good as he claimed, Ralph probably could be convinced to make it worth his while.

'I think we can convince Ralph to come up with some kind of legitimate settlement that will give you the security you're looking for,' Connie said. 'Now, I'd like to hear your story, and then we can decide how best to proceed.'

So for the next few hours, Bolt had related the events leading up to the moment when his world was shattered beyond redemption. No one, he assured them repeatedly, could have been aware he was in the adjoining darkened storage room, with the door ajar, during the final ugly confrontation. He had been coming down from a three-day binge and was lying on a cot in the little annex next to the Del Monaco conference room, trying to sweat it out before his next scheduled performance.

When angry voices exploded in the next room, he got quietly to his feet, tiptoed to the slightly open door and overheard every word that was spoken; saw every deed that transpired. Realizing his danger when at last the participants began to leave, he ducked down behind a storage cabinet, shaking in terror. But the door leading to his hiding place was never flung open, and eventually all was quiet in the outer room.

He immediately discarded the thought of going to the police. They would probably not believe him; and, in any case, he had no idea which of them might be on the take. He then thought about taking his story to some of the other family members — but that, too, was dangerous. The Del Monacos were a tight-knit bunch, and he knew without a doubt how much they would resist an outsider like himself interfering with 'family' business.

No. He knew instinctively that it was time for him to take his leave. He had been faltering in any case, with the drinking issue; and his boss, the hotel manager, probably would not be unhappy to get him off the payroll. He doubted any of the family, even Tommy, would ever notice he was gone. He packed his few belongings, cashed in his last voucher, got a bus ticket south, and headed back to New Orleans, where he still might be able to pick up a few side jobs.

'But how did you end up back here in Cathcart, of all places? Didn't you realize this was the Del Monacos' home turf?'

'I knew, but enough time had elapsed since those incidents that I thought I'd be in the clear. After all, it had been some time, and I hadn't talked to anyone at all about this, so why would they even think I might be a witness? I was offered a job at the hotel here and I needed it. I thought it was worth the risk.'

After some back and forth discussion, Gail and Connie made the decision to accept Clinton Bolt's story about the Del Monacos at face value. Hugo was commissioned to look into the details of the event Bolt had described and gain as much confirming information as possible about the individuals involved.

At the same time, an idea had formed in Gail's mind. 'Why don't we see if Charles can find a sober-living facility near Phoenix. We could put Bolt up there for a few weeks, and let him get some peace and quiet and decent meals out of harm's way. He wouldn't be as likely to come in contact with any of Tommy's associates out there, and he'd be rested and healthy by the time the case comes to trial. What do you all think?'

'That's a good idea, Gail,' Connie said. 'I'll contact Charles right away and see if he can look into the possibilities. In the meantime, Hugo, you or one of your people should be with him at all times as long as he's here, just for safety's sake.

'Is all this all right with you, Bolt?' he added, looking their witness squarely in the eye.

Bolt didn't flinch. 'That's fine with me. I could use a little R&R right about now.' He grinned and, for the first time since they had started the discussion, their new witness looked completely relaxed.

And so they had shipped him off to Charles, who got him set up at Rancho La Paz, a clean, quiet sober-living facility located about half an hour from Phoenix on the road toward the native ruins at Casa Grande. The United States Marshal

Service operating out of Phoenix agreed to check in on him several times a week, and Charles would fill in on their off days.

Bolt had settled into the relaxed pace of the ranch. The facility attendants reported he was quiet and cooperative, kept his private space neat and tidy, and appeared to have no problem adhering to their strict rules prohibiting drugs and alcohol on the premises, even though he steadily refused to take part in any of the group activities or sessions recommended by the facility.

Charles had relaxed a bit after the first few days. He had several conversations with the man, who seemed intelligent with a sense of humor, although somewhat terse and less than forthcoming about his personal life history beyond his experiences as a piano player in the entertainment industry.

Reflecting now about their decision, Connie had to admit that they just hadn't vetted Bolt thoroughly enough. Hugo had done the usual screening and background checks of course, but little of a substantive nature had turned up to explain why — and how — Bolt had become a key witness in a multi-million-dollar lawsuit.

Gail shook her head in frustration. She had come to the same conclusion and made a quick decision. 'We need to go back to our original defense strategy, Connie. The one thing we can't do now is put all our eggs in one basket and count on getting Bolt back in time to testify. I'm also wondering if this could have been some sort of set-up. After all, we have no proof that Tommy himself didn't lead us straight to Bolt then offer him cash to 'disappear'.'

'I've been thinking along those same lines myself,' Connie agreed. 'I'll get our team back on the defense strategy we had mapped out originally. We need to be prepared, however this plays out.'

'Right.'

Gail turned back to her computer and began typing in a series of triggers and reminders summarizing the various approaches to their original defense of Nino Del Monaco's will and Ralph's handling of his grandfather's estate.

Connie gave her a thumbs-up, and headed back to his office to confer with their associates about the new agenda. Change-up time!

5

Angus Shepherd, aka Clinton Bolt, strolled into a little cantina just off the Jardin area of San Miguel de Allende, in the heart of the Guanajuato mountain region of interior Mexico. It was midday and the place was nearly empty. Lazy flies circled near the open entrance, illuminated by bright rays of sunlight slanting in off the cobblestoned street. A couple of figures sat hunched over the bar, indistinguishable from lumpy potato sacks. Bolt couldn't tell if they were male or female, nor did he care much. He strolled past the bar and the few sunny tables near the front, choosing instead a small vinyl-covered booth deep in the bowels of the dimly lit interior.

'*Hola*.' The short, chubby *Mozo* swiped a grungy cloth over the table, dispelling a few crumbs and damp spots. '*¿Cerveza?*'

'No.' The thought of beer this early in the morning turned his stomach. He was tempted to ask for a shot of tequila, but resisted.

'*Huevos y papas, por favor. Y café . . . muchos café.*' A good solid breakfast of fried eggs and potatoes, washed down with steaming cups of hot black coffee, were what he needed right now.

'*Si, Señor.*'

He sat there a bit, watching the tourists outside. They looked like exotic birds in their brightly patterned clothing. Their progress through the quaint streets was hampered by clunky totes and cameras that hung around their necks like harnesses. They ambled along, chirping to each other and taking in the sights. How long ago had it been since he had been that carefree and naïve? It seemed like an eternity.

A shadow crossed his line of sight and he looked up. 'Hello,' he said. 'What took you so long?'

She sat the tray down with a 'thump' and placed the plate of food in front of him. '*¿Café?*'

He nodded and watched as she poured the hot black liquid into a chunky earthenware mug. '*Gracias.*'

'*De nada.*'

She started to turn away and he held up a hand. 'Have a seat.'

'Can't,' she said. '*Mozo* will have a fit.'

'He won't mind. It's not that busy. Come on, take a load off. I've got a proposition for you.'

She glanced back at the barman, saw he was involved in a conversation with one of the bar denizens, and shrugged. 'All right. Don't mind if I do.' She watched as he tore a corn tortilla in half and sopped up some of the egg yolk with it. 'I didn't know you were back. You still at the same place?'

'No,' he lied evenly. 'I've got a gig going down in Mexico City. I'm just up for the day to tie up some loose ends.'

'What kind of proposition?' She eyed him suspiciously as he shoveled in the hot food.

'Nothing heavy. Can you still go back and forth across the border?'

'Last time I checked.'

'I've got a package I need delivered to Laredo. It would just be a quick trip. I'll pay all your expenses and the usual fee as well.'

'A package? I don't want to be carrying no dope, Angus. The last time I did that for some freak I nearly got caught. Scared the hell outta me.'

'Naw, it's nothing like that. Just a message, really. I don't want to trust it to the mail. You just take the bus up there, deliver the packet to a courier service, have a nice dinner or something, and head on back. That's all there is to it. There's nothing illegal about it.'

'Why can't you take it up there yourself?'

'I told you. I got a gig going. I don't have the time to do it myself.'

He pushed his plate back.

The remnants of grease reflected the one sunny ray of sunlight streaming down on the table. One of the flies circled and came in for a landing.

'Look,' he said, laying a few *pesos* down. 'If you don't want to do it, just say so. You ain't the only fish in the sea, Lila.'

She recoiled, as if he had slapped her, hard, across the face. 'No, no. I'm not turning it down. I just want to be sure it's not too risky. I can't afford to do any time.' She looked as if she might start crying.

He looked at her closely. He hoped she wasn't using again. 'All right,' he said finally. 'I'll be back in a day or two, with the packet and your dough. You be ready, and be sure to tell ol' *mozo* you're going to have to take a day off toward the end of the week. *¿Comprendes?*'

'*Si*. I'll be ready. And, Angus?'

'Yes?'

'Thanks. I'll do a good job for you, I promise.'

'I know you will, Lila. You're a good kid.'

He took one last sip of coffee, stood, turned his back on her, and strolled out into the bright sunlight.

Just another day in paradise.

6

On my way to paradise, Hugo thought, buckling up for the through flight to Phoenix. He glanced at Jake Morrow, who was gazing out the window as the plane taxied down the runway. 'You ever been to Arizona?'

'Nope. Never been west of the Mississippi, as a matter of fact. This will be new territory for me.' He smiled happily. 'I'm looking forward to the change of scenery.'

Hugo nodded. He liked Jake. The young man had started out his career with the Cathcart Police Department. Like Hugo, he came from a long line of law enforcement professionals. His father, Asa Morrow, had once been chief with the department, and Jake had hoped to make a name there for himself as well. As time went by, however, the eager young patrolman became increasingly disillusioned with the bureaucratic hierarchy.

One day he had had enough. Hugo received a call that evening from his own father, Hugo, Sr., a long-time friend of Asa Morrow's.

'Son,' his father said in that familiar growl, 'do you think you might have room to take on a new project?'

'What kind of project?' Hugo, Jr. replied cautiously. 'Depends on what it is.'

'I'd like you to consider giving Asa's son Jake a look-see. He's gotten pretty discouraged down there at the department. He might be looking to make a career change. Thought you might be able to give him some pointers.'

'Sure, Dad. I'd be glad to talk to him. Don't know if I can make room for him right now, but I might be able to give him some suggestions and encouragement.'

Jake Morrow had come to Hugo's office the very next day. After talking to the young man for a bit, Hugo knew right away he had possibilities. He had taken his police training seriously and knew quite a bit about law and procedure. He was smart as a whip, but pleasant and respectful as well.

'I can offer you a beginning position here, if you're interested,' Hugo said finally, leaning back in his desk chair. 'It won't be a lot of money at first, but if you're diligent and apply yourself, there's room for advancement for you. Several of my older operatives will be thinking of retirement soon. I might as well be prepared for that . . . whenever it happens.'

Jake, serious up until then, had smiled broadly. 'I accept, Mr. Goldthwaite! How soon can I start?'

'Better give the department a decent notice, Jake. No point in getting their dander up or making unnecessary enemies there. How about two weeks from next Monday? That will give me a chance to make room for you here.' He glanced around at the crowded work space, with tables and desks lined up along the walls and down the center of the room, then turned to the young man. 'By the way, you'd better call me Hugo. Mr. Goldthwaite's my father.' He smiled back at his new hire.

'That's great Mr. er . . . Hugo! I'm really looking forward to this opportunity!'

And now here they were, some six months later, on their way to Jake's first big op. Hugo hoped he hadn't dropped this assignment on Jake too quickly after the young man's change of career. But at least he would be there to oversee the operation.

He wasn't quite sure what to expect either, once they got to the ranch outside of Phoenix. But at least he would have backup; and Jake was strong, well-trained in the use of firearms. He was a martial arts expert too, which made him even more valuable. Hugo hoped they wouldn't need those kinds of skills for this job, but it was just as well to go in prepared for the worst-case scenario.

'Here we go,' he said as the pilot began his incline. 'Off into the wild blue yonder.'

7

'Thanks for coming in on such short notice, Ralph.' Gail ushered her client in to her office. 'Would you like some coffee?' she added, gesturing at the bar in the corner.

'No, I'm fine,' he said, taking a seat in front of her desk. 'What's all this about, Gail? I was worried when I got your message.'

'I might as well give it to you straight, Ralph. Clinton Bolt has disappeared.'

Ralph Del Monaco heaved a sigh. 'Do you have any idea what happened to him?'

'Not yet. Hugo's on his way out there. Oh, I don't think we ever told you where he was staying?'

Ralph shook his head.

'Charles was looking after him out in Phoenix,' she went on. 'We had put him up at a sober-living facility just outside Casa Grande. By all accounts, he was doing fine there.'

'And what happened to him? Do you think there's any possibility Tommy got wind of all this? I'd hate to think . . . '

'Early days, Ralph, early days. Let's wait until Hugo makes an assessment before we jump to conclusions. He may have gotten cold feet and left on his own hook. I'm not willing to believe Tommy would be so blatant as to have him snatched. Not yet, anyway.'

'So what do we do if we don't find him . . . in time for the trial, I mean?'

'Connie and I are already working on that. You know we'd already worked up a defense strategy before Bolt came on the scene. As you know, his testimony was so compelling that it led us to change our approach and focus on the new information. But we still have all of the original defense plan saved up. It's a very simple matter to present your case just as we were going to present it originally — if that strategy is still all right with you, of course.'

'You and Connie are the experts, Gail. I'm way out of my depth when it comes

46

to defense strategies.' He managed a tight little smile.

'Good. That's basically what I wanted to hear from you today, Ralph. I need your permission to present the case as we had discussed in the beginning. You realize, of course, we would have had not only a stronger case with Bolt's testimony, but there was also the element of surprise.' She paused. 'We really were assuming Tommy didn't know Bolt was listening in that night. And we were hoping his surprise testimony would catch your relatives unawares. Now we have to assume that maybe the cat's already out of the bag. I hope not, but it's a possibility that they know all about Bolt and his story. In fact, they may have known all along.'

'And if they did know or find out, they could have trailed him to Phoenix and . . . '

'Right. They could have taken him out of the equation or, even more likely, they could have paid him off to just disappear. In either case, he's gone now; and unless we find him in the next month, his testimony against your uncles is gone, too.'

Ralph stood up and walked over to the window and gazed out at Main Street. 'Damn! I didn't know the guy very well, but he always seemed like the harmless type. I'd sure hate to think that he's come to mischief on my account.'

'But it wasn't on *your* account, Ralph. He was looking for a payday, you know that. He wanted to get as much as he could in return for telling his story in court. Whatever's happened to him, it has nothing to do with you, and you are definitely not to blame for any of this.'

'Thanks, Gail,' he said, returning to his seat. 'I needed to hear that, I guess. I think Nino would be turning over in his grave right now if he knew how all this was affecting the family. God knows I didn't want any of this to happen. Sometimes I think it might be better just to give up and turn everything over to them. It would sure be a lot easier.'

'That's not how Nino wanted it, Ralph. And he told you that. Your grandfather picked you because he believed you would do the right thing. It's obvious, if Bolt's story is accurate, that Tommy and the others have a very different take on what the 'right thing' is. If Nino is rolling over in his grave, it's more likely because of Tommy's actions — not yours.'

She drew a hefty file folder towards her, pulled out a few papers and handed them to Ralph. 'Now let's go over these documents one more time. We need to get back up to speed on your original defense, just in case. If Hugo can find Bolt and convince him to come back, we'll go with his story as we planned. Otherwise, it's back to square one again.'

8

Lila Moran woke with a start. The *Americanos* jitney was pulling into one of the border checkpoints between the Mexican city of Nuevo Laredo and Laredo, Texas just the other side of the Rio Grande.

She smoothed her hair and pulled out her papers. This was the tricky part. She had kept up her US citizenship, even though she had spent a number of the past few years living and working in San Miguel. She knew that was the main reason Angus had asked her to make this run. Everything depended on getting into Laredo, making the drop, and getting back across the border into Nuevo Laredo without a hitch.

She was tired, even with the fits and starts of sleep she'd managed over the ten-hour ride. The bus was comfortable enough, for what it was, but it made unscheduled stops every so often along the way to pick up little groups of people standing alongside the road, waiting for a ride into the next town.

'¿Documentos? Papers?' The Border Patrol agent paused next to her seat. Without comment, she handed him her passport and I.D. She tried to look bored as he scanned the paperwork, looking back and forth from the photo to her face. 'Do you live in the States?'

'Not at the moment. I've been working in San Miguel, at a tourist facility. I'm meeting some of my relatives in Laredo for a little family get-together,' she lied. She had rehearsed this bit to get just the right feeling of nonchalance. 'It's my grandfather's birthday tomorrow.'

She could tell he had suddenly lost interest in her, her family and her grandfather, the birthday boy. Expats visiting and working in San Miguel were commonplace, and traveled back and forth frequently. He handed back her papers without further comment and moved on down the aisle.

Wide awake now, she gazed out the window as the bus started up again to make the trek on into town and the bus terminal. Her aim was to get in and out of Laredo as quickly as possible. She would take an afternoon bus out, if she could, hopefully making it back into San Miguel by early tomorrow morning. With any luck, she could get to the cantina in time to pull her shift without risking *Mozo*'s anger at taking more than one day off.

The bus ambled on into Laredo, taking its sweet time, stopping at every corner and light it seemed. She drummed her fingers impatiently on the vinyl arm rest, humming an aimless little tune to herself.

She had once been a singer of sorts. That was how she and Angus had met, in some long-forgotten cantina, long ago. Now her voice was gone, ruined with too much tequila and too many cigarettes — and she was waiting tables in a bar. What a change that was.

Finally they coasted to a stop at one of the off-loading points. She was ready with her little tote, carried mainly to look as if she were making a legitimate visit, her papers, and spare cash now carefully stashed away in a money belt double-hooked to her bra for extra security.

She stood, swaying gently as the bus made its final stop, then made her way down the aisle to exit.

'*Buenas dias!*' called out the driver, as he did to every passable woman departing his chariot. She ignored him, scuttled down the steps, and hurried through the doors into the terminal. She made a fast stop in the lavatory to use the facilities and quickly check her appearance in the spotted mirror. Then she was out the door and on to the street, looking for a cab.

She was in luck. One pulled into the space next to her, and she quickly opened the door and hopped in. She gave the driver an address out on Highway 35 towards the airport. She wasn't too surprised when they pulled up to a rib place. The tantalizing smell of barbecue rose from several big black smokers at the back of the parking lot.

'You sure this is the right place, lady?' The cab driver looked suspiciously at the half-empty lot.

'Yes, I'm sure. Could you wait for me, though? I'll pay you double.'

'Sure. I don't mind. Take your time.' He shut off the motor, lit a cigarette, and pulled out a magazine.

'Thanks. I won't be long.' *I hope*, she thought.

She was relieved when she entered. It was, indeed, a barbecue rib joint and tavern, as advertised. But she could see at the back of the place what looked to be a large office area, separated from the eatery by large plate-glass windows. Inside, several burly men sat at desks, staring intently at computer screens or scribbling feverishly on lined yellow pads. A bank of what looked like postal boxes lined the back wall.

Lila made her way past the bar, ignoring the questioning glance of a lone bus boy scrubbing the floor, and rapped at the door to the office area. The nearest man looked up. Seeing nothing to alarm him, he nodded, pressed a buzzer, and gestured for her to enter.

'What can I do you for you?' he said, turning his computer screen off. He indicated she could have a seat at his desk.

'I need to leave a parcel with you for transfer,' she said evenly. She pulled out the little packet Angus had given her, with the instructions and address clearly marked in black ink on the brown paper covering.

The man took it from her, looked it over carefully, then pulled a loose-leaf log from a drawer. He thumbed through to find the right page and scanned back and forth between the log and the packet. 'This looks all right to me. That's a valid address for here. Got all the right markings.' He nodded over at the postal boxes. 'That'll be $50 — cash.' He glanced up at her to see how she would take the news.

She was prepared. Angus had told her that would be the fee, and he had given her enough cash to cover all her expenses, including the bus and taxi fares. She had put two twenties and a ten in the top of her bra in the restroom at the bus station. Now she pulled out the bills and handed them to him. 'I'm to get a receipt,' she said.

'Of course.' He wrote something down on the packet, put the log back and pulled out a small receipt book. 'Here you go, little lady. Pleasure doing business with you.'

'Thank you,' she said, folding the receipt and tucking it into her bra where the money had been. She rose, nodded to him, and made her way back out through the restaurant and into the heat of the parking lot beyond. It was over 100 degrees today, and she could feel the perspiration filming her forehead and dampening her clothes.

She climbed back into the waiting taxi and directed the driver to take her back to the bus terminal, hopefully in time to catch the early bus back to San Miguel.

She had no idea what she had just delivered, or what it all meant. The most important thing to her was the $500 USD Angus had promised her to make this trip. That would pay for a lot of *frijoles* over the next few months.

She was like one of those little gray

squirrels, she thought, laughing silently to herself. *My cheeks are full of nuts now, all stored up for winter!*

9

While Lila Moran made her way back across the Mexican border to Nuevo Laredo and points south, Hugo Goldthwaite and Jake Morrow were speeding south from Phoenix to Casa Grande and Rancho La Paz. They had no idea what they would find there, but since that was the last known sighting for their quarry, Clinton Bolt, they would follow protocol and attempt to start tracking him from there.

Upon arrival, they were ushered in to a roomy public area, pleasantly cool and closed off from the hot Arizona sun beating down on the harsh desert landscape outside. 'Would you like something cool to drink?' the young woman asked.

'Yes, that would be great,' Hugo responded for the both of them. They weren't used to the heat, and it would be important to remember to stay hydrated while they were here.

'I'll get Miz Meecher for you. She's expecting you.'

Jake and Hugo took their seats. A few minutes later, the door reopened and a smiling middle-aged woman entered, followed by the attendant with tall glasses of ice water. There was the usual flurry of introductions, followed by the settling down again with their drinks, before the older woman addressed the topic.

'I'm so very sorry Mr. Bolt decided to leave us when he did,' she said. 'We thought he was doing fine, but . . . ' She hesitated. 'Sometimes the pressure to do well just becomes too great for some of our people. Mr. Bolt was a quiet man. He didn't want to take part in any of the group sessions. Perhaps if he had . . . '

'I'm sure it was not anything to do with your facility that inspired Mr. Bolt to leave the way he did, Mrs. Meecher,' Hugo said. 'He may have just decided he needed a — a change of scenery.'

'Perhaps.' She waited a moment while Hugo took another sip of the cool water.

'However, there is something else which may be of help . . . '

'We would be glad of any assistance you could provide, ma'am. We really are anxious to get in touch with Mr. Bolt . . . and help him take care of any issues he may be trying to resolve.'

'Well, there *is* another gentleman staying here who had a bit of contact with him. He came to our board last evening and said he might have some information about why Mr. Bolt left as he did, and possibly an idea about where he might have gone.'

'That's very good news. That's just the kind of feedback we've been hoping for. Would this gentleman be willing to speak with us?'

'Oh, I'm sure he would. He seemed most eager to shed what little light he could on the subject of Mr. Bolt's whereabouts. Would you like to see him now? I think he's in his room.'

'That would be great if we could speak with him. And thank you so much for your hospitality,' Hugo added.

Mrs. Meecher rose and gestured

toward the door. 'You're entirely welcome, gentlemen. This way, if you please. Mr. Rowe's room is just down the hall here to your right.'

Standing aside so Hugo and Jake could enter the private room, she said, 'Mr. Rowe, these gentlemen are here to talk to you about Mr. Bolt. Do you mind?'

'No, not at all. C'mon in, gents. Make yerselves at home.'

The speaker was a grizzled little man seated in a recliner pulled near the window looking out on the desert and mountains beyond. There was a bit of to-do about getting chairs pulled around in a circle, and general introductions were made.

'Now, fellers,' Rowe said, 'what kin I do y' fer?'

Hugo digested this last bit and nodded. 'Thanks, Mr. Rowe, for seeing us today. We understand you were friends with Mr. Bolt — '

'Henry. Call me Henry. Naw, I wasn't whatcha could call 'friends' with old Bolt. More like 'quaintances.''

'But you did have some conversations

with him from time to time? Mrs. Meecher says — '

'Oh, yessir, we did have.' The old man cackled and cleared his throat.

For one awful moment Hugo thought Henry might actually hack up a gob of tobacco juice and unload it on Mrs. Meecher's fake magenta 'Oriental' rug manufactured in a sweatshop somewhere in China. He didn't, though, and after a brief bout of coughing relieved by a swig from his water bottle, he continued.

'Ol' Bolt was an interestin' feller, all right. We talked a bit from time to time, mostly about the good ol' days. He was in show business, y' know. A piano player. Said he'd played all over the place — Vegas, N'awlins and all. Had quite the life, I guess.'

'Did he ever tell you he was planning to leave the ranch?'

'Well, now, not in so many words. 'Course all us ol' geezers think we're gonna get outta here, sooner or later. Fer most of us, it's gonna be later . . . feet first.' He cackled again at the little joke he'd made.

Hugo smiled. 'Yes, but did he ever say anything specifically? Like when he might leave — and where he might go?'

'Hmm?' Henry scratched the gray stubble on his chin, reached over and grabbed the water bottle for another swig. 'Y' know, it would sure be nice if I had a wee bit of cash to hand, fer cigarettes and such. Y' know, walkin'-around money.'

Hugo had expected this, and spoke quickly and directly to the old man. 'That can be arranged, Henry. But first we have to have something to work with. Did Bolt actually say anything at all about where he might be headed once he left here?'

Henry pondered this a moment, then straightened up. 'The only thin' he ever said about any place in perticular was when he got to talkin' about his gramma and gramps.'

'What do you mean?'

'Well, he was downright proud of his folks. Spoke quite highly of 'em. Said as how they was missionaries of sorts, people that went around different places and spoke about God to the natives and such.'

'And?' Hugo was beginning to think this was a dead-end street. He glanced over at Jake, who was scribbling away as fast as he could, taking down the conversation on his yellow legal pad. 'And how did that lead into him telling you where he was headed?'

'Well, not in so many words . . . But what he *did* say was his people went down into Méjico in the early days. Spent quite a bit of time down there, they did. Learned the lingo real well.' He glanced out the window at two men clearing weeds on the other side of the patio before continuing. 'Claimed that was how he learned it, too — the lingo I mean. Learned it from them, his gran'parents. And he could speak it pretty good, too, fer a *gringo*. I'd see him out there in the yard, yakkin' away like a jaybird with them yard guys.' He nodded toward the men outside. 'And Camila, the lady who cooks fer us? He'd talk her up a storm, about the food and how good it was an' all. She lapped that up, she did. Snuck special treats into his room alla time. It were real funny, how he had her wrapped around his li'l finger. Yep, he musta been a real ladies' man in the day, all right.'

This revelation called for another round of hacking and a few sips at the water bottle. When Henry Rowe had settled down once more, Hugo began again. 'So what you're saying . . . what I think you're saying . . . is that you think he might have headed south — maybe as far as Mexico?'

'I think it's a good possibility. Mind you, he never *said* anythin' like that fer sure. But the way he went on about Mé-*ji*co this and Mé-*ji*co that, I got the feelin' he'd spent some time there himself. I could be wrong about that, 'course. It's just a feelin' I got. Sometimes those feelin's is worth more than a sure thing.'

Hugo allowed that he did indeed know about the validity of such feelings. He was just about to wrap up their talk and pay off the old coot when Henry suddenly slapped his thigh.

'Dang! I just almost fergot the most important *thing*!'

'You've remembered something else?'

Hugo felt that familiar jolt of adrenaline — the rush he got when some new piece of the puzzle was revealed to him.

'Mind now, I can't say fer sure this means anythin' at all. But it might . . . yes, indeedy, it might mean *sumthin'*.'

'Believe me, Mr., er, Henry, anything that might help would be most welcome.' Jake sat next to him, poised, his felt-tip pen hovering over the yellow blue-lined paper.

'Well, this happened just a day or two before Bolt took off. It was about this time of day, too, so the shadows were startin' to get a bit long out there, just like that.' He gestured out toward the patio and desert landscape beyond. The normally brown mountainside in the distance was beginning to turn a garish pinkish-orange from the slanting rays of the setting sun.

'Go on,' Hugo urged.

'Bolt had been on one of his strolls, takin' a turn around the yard an' all. Camila had come lookin' fer us, callin' us in fer our eats. She asked me to go out and see if I cud round up ol' Bolt, and I said, 'Sure, be glad to,' so out I headed. Just when I got to the doorway leadin' out from the main room . . . ' He glanced at Hugo, who nodded — yes, he knew where that was. ' . . . just then I got sight of ol' Bolt. He was standin' out there just this side of the cottonwood tree. That thing is huge, with a trunk as big as a barrel. An' Bolt was just standin' there, this side of it, lookin' 'round it at the street.'

'The street? What was he looking at? Could you tell?'

'That's just it. There weren't nothin' *there*. Leastways, there weren't nothin' there *at first*. An' that's when I heard it.'

'Heard it? Heard what?'

'It was a car motor comin' down that road, at quite a clip from the sound of it. Bolt heard it, too. I could tell by the way he was standin' there, his ear cocked. I stayed back inside the doorway a bit, so no one could see me, even if they looked over towards the house.

'Now here's the funny bit. Just when that car rolled up over that rise out there — ' He gestured. ' — just then, that car come to a complete stop, right out there in the road in front of the sign that says 'Rancho La Paz.' An' it didn't move none. Just sat there, with that engine purrin' like a big ol' jungle cat.'

'What did Bolt do then?'

'Bolt just stood there, smack up against that cottonwood tree trunk, and waited it out. That car sat there for the longest time, motor runnin' an' all, like it was makin' up its mind to come on in or not.'

'Could you tell what make of car it was?'

'Well, now, I ain't so good on makes of cars, 'specially the new ones. Besides, I was hangin' back inside the door so *I* couldn't be seen neither. What I *can* tell you is, it was one of them long, low types. Black an' a sedan. That's about all I can tell you about it.'

'And it left without coming in?'

'Yep. It hunkered down there for a while — probably not as long as it seemed like; then it revved up that motor again, turned around right there in the middle of the road, an' scooted on back up the hill towards Phoenix. Never stopped, an' never come back, not so fer as I know.'

'What did Bolt do then?'

'He stayed right where he was fer a piece. After a bit, after that devil car had been gone a while, I called out to him that Camila wanted us to come in fer eats. He eased out from behind that tree, gave a look-see up the road — to be sure, I guess, that the thing were gone — then came on in to eat, natural as you like. He never said nothin' about that car, an' I didn't ask him neither.'

'And you say he left the ranch not long afterwards?'

'Yep. It wasn't a day or two an' he lit out. Got up one mornin' an' he'd flown the coop. Miz Meecher an' all were mighty upset about it, too. Then, of course, when the rest of them guys showed up . . . '

'You mean the US Marshals?'

'Yep, an' that attorney feller with 'em. When *they* showed up, well then, all *hell* broke loose. Pardon my French, young feller.' He nodded at Jake, who looked up from his notepad and smiled. 'Yep, that were an *interestin'* mornin', if I do say so.'

'So you never saw Bolt again after that?'

'Nope. That feller were *gone*. He'd cleared out, kit an' caboodle, sometime before dawn. They went out an' looked high an' low fer him, of course. But there weren't no trace of the guy. He just vanished into thin air.'

Hugo pondered the old man's story and wondered about its accuracy. Still, there was no good reason for Henry Rowe to lie about it. He thanked the man for his cooperation, pressed a $100 bill into his hand, and he and Jake left the room.

Henry smiled to himself as he tucked the C-note away in his hidey-hole, right next to the one Bolt had given him to keep his damned mouth shut, just before making his getaway. He'd probably never see Bolt again and, with any luck, that crazy old piano player would never be the wiser.

The mountains in the distance were now ablaze with color from the setting sun. The old cottonwood tree cast a long shadow across the dry brown yard. If he scrunched up his eyes a bit, Henry could still see Bolt crouched out there, hiding from the devil car.

It gave him the shivers.

10

Later that evening Hugo called Gail.

'How's it going?' she asked.

'I don't think we're going to find him in time for the trial. Just wanted to give you a heads-up on that.'

'Have you got any ideas?' Gail motioned to Connie and hit the speaker button so he could hear what Hugo was saying.

'Nothing concrete. I'm beginning to believe he left of his own volition, however. There's one odd bit — several, actually. But all indications are that he took off under his own steam.'

'What's the odd bit?' Gail asked. Maybe if they all put their heads together they could figure this out.

'A day or so before Bolt took off, one of the guys here who had gotten friendly with him witnessed him apparently hiding from a car that pulled up out in front of the place. He said the car sat there for a while idling, then turned around and went back where it came from. Two mornings later, Bolt was missing at dawn. Looks like he packed his bag and took off in the middle of the night. I have no idea how he made his getaway. The ranch isn't near any public transportation, and Bolt didn't have a car.'

'Could someone have picked him up? Doesn't seem likely he would have been up to a long hike.'

'He might have hitchhiked. That's a regular truck route through there, heading down to Tucson. He could have hid alongside of the road and just waited until a likely ride came along.'

'That sounds plausible. But why? Do you think he was afraid some of Tommy's men were in that car? Did the friend get any kind of description or license number?'

'His description of the car would fit every other car on the road. And no, he didn't get a number. Fact is, the old guy was kind of cagey. He could have been leading us on at Bolt's instigation.'

'Hmm.' Gail glanced at Connie, who

whispered something. She nodded and continued: 'Did this man have any idea at all where Bolt might have been headed?'

'Well, that's the interesting part. He made quite a point — went on and on, as a matter of fact — about Bolt's ties to Mexico. Seems his grandparents had lived there for a while, years ago, and even taught him the language as he was growing up.'

'That's interesting. Any idea what part of Mexico?'

'None. Just that they had lived there, liked it, and passed on some of that sentiment to Bolt.'

'Well, that would be like looking for a needle in the proverbial haystack. I don't suppose there'd be any point in checking with some of the Border Patrol people?'

'Problem is, Gail, he's probably using a different name by now,' said Connie, 'and he may have altered his appearance. With the traffic going back and forth across those checkpoints, I doubt anyone would remember him at all. No, I think we have to accept that he's gone, and I don't see much value in spending more time on it. I wish I could be more positive, but I think it would be a fool's errand.'

'All right.' She glanced again at Connie, who nodded. 'Connie's here and he agrees with you. You and Jake better pack it in and head on back. I know you've got work to do here. No point in beating a dead horse.'

'If I thought there was any possibility of actually finding the guy any time soon, I'd hang on a bit longer. At least Charles is here. If anything does change or we get new information, he'll be able to follow up on this end. I hate to give up — goes against the grain, y' know — but I don't know what else to do here.'

'Let us know if anything changes. Otherwise, we'll expect you back here in Cathcart in a day or so. Give Charles our best. None of this was his fault, and I don't want him to waste any more time or effort on it.'

'Okay. I think we'll get a good night's sleep tonight and try to catch the first flight out tomorrow. The thought of a red-eye doesn't exactly thrill me. I'll let you know if that changes for any reason.'

'Have a good trip. By the way, could you settle up with the people at the ranch for us? That was a waste of time and effort, but at least we gave it a try.'

'I already did that, Gail. I figured that even if we do find Bolt, there's no way he's going back to the ranch. If I get my hands on him, I'll drag him back to Cathcart — kicking and screaming, if necessary.'

Gail thanked Hugo and clicked off the line. She met Connie's gaze across the table. 'I wonder just where in Mexico Mr. Bolt is right now,' she said. 'I'd give a pretty penny to know what that's all about.'

11

Lila Moran made it back to the cantina the next day, just in time for opening. She was a bit hungover from the long bus trip, but concealed it with an upper and plenty of makeup. *Mozo* nodded when he saw she'd opened up, started the big coffee urn, and had begun to sweep the pavement in front of the establishment.

'*Bueno*' he said, half in greeting and half in grudging approval.

'*Bueno*' she responded automatically. She had offered no explanation for her request for a day off, and he had not asked. In their world, you never asked a question you did not already know the answer to.

She had no idea if Angus would show up today, or even if she would ever see him again. She did not know where he was staying now, nor could she remember where he had been staying when she first met him. Their history together was spotty and limited to the various hang-outs and bars in the seedier sections of San Miguel or Mexico City, where he had been playing gigs at the same time she was either singing or waiting on tables. It wasn't a lot to go on. On the plus side, the one-day trip to Laredo hadn't cost her anything, and she even had scrimped on the costs a bit, so she still had some of the expense money he had advanced her. So it was a win-win situation, more or less.

If he actually showed up and came through with the $500 as he'd promised, it would be all to the good. If not, she wasn't really out anything except the day of lost work — no big thing. Still, she had no reason to think Angus would screw her. She'd first met him years ago, and she'd never known him to welch on anything or go back on his word. But they both lived on the edge. It was conceivable that he might get into a situation that would make it impossible for him to meet his obligation to her. If so, she would forgive him. But she would be less likely to trust him in the future. Your word was only as good as the last time you gave it.

She had learned that lesson the hard way, and it was one she was not liable to forget.

'*¿Cómo 'stá?*'

She hadn't seen him enter. He was like that, appearing and disappearing without a sound. Like a ghost, really.

'*Muy bien. ¿Y tú?*'

'I'm all right. How was your trip?'

'The trip went fine . . . ' She hesitated. She didn't know if she should just hand him the receipt for the packet transfer, or wait for him to ask.

He went on back and took a seat in an empty booth. He glanced at *Mozo* and held up two fingers. The barman nodded. He poured two ounces of tequila into a shot glass, uncapped an icy *cerveza*, plunked them on a round tray and gestured to Lila.

She carried the drinks back to Angus's booth and set them down, leaving the little change tray on the table next to them.

'Sit down,' he said.

This time she didn't bother looking at *Mozo*. She watched as he took a sip of the fiery liqueur, followed by a slug of beer. He looked at her. 'Well?'

'Like I said, it all went down just as you said it would.' She looked around. Again, the bar was half-empty. Nobody was looking at them. 'Here,' she added, pulling the wrinkled receipt out of her bra and handing it to him. It was still damp from her perspiration.

He unfolded it and laid it out on the table, carefully avoiding the circles of liquid left by previous glasses. He inspected it thoroughly, folded it back up and put it into his shirt pocket. 'You did good, Lila. You did real good.'

She relaxed a little, relieved that the receipt was acceptable. She didn't say anything, not daring to bring up the topic of the fee.

But she needn't have worried. He reached into his back pocket and pulled out a plain white envelope, and handed it to her. She didn't insult him by opening it to check the contents, but folded it in thirds and stuffed it down in the top of her damp bra where the receipt had recently resided. 'Thanks,

Angus. I appreciate — '

'*De nada*,' he said, smiling. 'I think we're straight now, aren't we, Lila?'

'Yes.' She nodded, moving to stand up.

Suddenly, like a snake, he reached out across the table and grabbed her wrist. Alarmed, she looked at him in apprehension. 'Now. You haven't seen me, Lila. In fact, you don't *know* me. *¿Comprendes?*'

'*Si, te entiendo.*' She nodded vigorously. 'I haven't seen you at all.'

'And if someone comes around here asking about me, you don't know nothin'.'

'No, I swear.'

'And if you see me out in the street anywhere, either here in S.M. or down in Mexico D.F., you're not going to recognize me, *are you?*'

His grip on her wrist tightened. She'd have a bruise there tomorrow. 'No, Angus, I swear. I don't know you . . . I *won't* know you if I see you. I promise!'

She was frightened now. He was still smiling at her, just like always — but his blue eyes were cold and vacant, just like a lizard's eyes, or those of a snake.

81

He released her wrist and she jumped up and fled to the back of the bar. *Mozo* eyed her curiously. The next time Lila Moran dared to look up, Angus Shepherd was gone.

12

Gail gazed at Connie over her coffee cup. The two of them sat in comfortable silence, finishing breakfast and gearing up to face another challenging day at the firm.

She treasured this quiet part of the morning, just the two of them. She often wondered how she had coped with life and all its ups and downs before Conrad Osterlitz had entered her world. Everything had changed after that. No matter how difficult the task, with Connie at her side she was up to everything life had to throw at her — including this latest fiasco with their missing witness, Clinton Bolt.

Hugo and Jake would be flying in from Phoenix later this afternoon, and she was looking forward to getting together with them and picking their brains. Hugo had said he thought they should move forward with their original line of defense, since he saw no hope of tracking down the elusive Bolt and dragging him back in. But she couldn't help but wonder if he was right about that.

There was probably good reason to just let it go, she thought. A reluctant witness was often more detrimental to a case than no witness at all. And no matter what Bolt's reasons were for fleeing, if he had second thoughts about testifying against his former bosses, they and Ralph Del Monaco were probably better off without him. She didn't like surprises, and in her experience putting someone on the stand who didn't want to be there was tantamount to a disastrous outcome. Furthermore, she and Connie owed Ralph the best possible defense they could muster. Trying to shoehorn in Clinton Bolt's testimony, no matter how valuable it looked on the surface, could result in a nasty surprise.

No, she grudgingly admitted. It was far better to gear up to present the more mundane case and hope for the best, than to push a reluctant Bolt into saying something damaging, no matter how compelling his original tale had seemed.

After all, they didn't know this man; he had just shown up out of the blue. What was it Hugo had said? One of his street informants had contacted him about 'some guy with some information you might find interesting.'

Odd. And far too convenient. The more she thought about it, the more convinced she became that Bolt had been put up for this job. It wasn't too much of a stretch to think that Tommy Del Monaco and his boys already had paid Bolt off. The whole thing could have been a scam to discredit Ralph. And Bolt's sudden departure could have been part of the plan as well.

Suddenly restless, she gathered their dishes and rinsed them for the dishwasher. 'Do you have to be in court again this morning?' she asked. Connie had an ongoing trial that was dragging on with no end in sight.

'Yeah.' He sighed, put down the newspaper he'd been scanning and looked at her, sensing her restlessness. 'Why don't you go out to your mother's for a while today? You haven't seen them yet this week. Maybe Erle would fancy a walk.'

'I was thinking the same thing.' Erle was her brother with special needs. She had always been close to him, and tried to carry some of the load of his care for her widowed mother. Alberta Norris was getting on in years, and after a crisis of sorts last year, they had all agreed to some lifestyle changes.

Alberta's younger cousin, Lucy Verner, a retired nurse, had made the decision to give up her home in the northern part of the state and move in with Alberta and Erle to help ease the situation. Erle, who had gradually gotten more and more difficult to control, had undergone in-depth testing to determine what the best course of treatment for him might be. After a brief stay in a private facility, and a correction of his medications, they had all been thankful to see him blossom into a better-functioning individual. Gone were the frequent tantrums and uncontrollable outbursts. The combination of the new prescriptions and Lucy's competent and loving care had made a world of difference — in all their lives.

'All right,' Gail said, wiping her hands. 'I think I'll do just that — take a run out to Mother's and catch up with her and Lucy. And yes, I think a walk with Erle would do us both some good.'

'Fine. I think that's perfect. Once Hugo and Jake get back, I suspect we're going to be tied up for the rest of the week, getting back to the basics in our defense plan for Ralph. You might as well take advantage of the few hours you have between now and the meeting this afternoon. Clear the cobwebs!'

Later, as she drove over the familiar streets to Long Hills, the upscale subdivision where her family had lived from her birth, she still couldn't help thinking about Clinton Bolt. Who was he, really? And what kind of a game was he trying to play with them?

'Hi, all,' she called as she entered the Norris vestibule.

'Out here, Gail,' sang out Lucy. 'We're out here in the sunroom. Grab a cup of coffee if you want. I think there's still some left in the pot.'

Gail placed her bag on the table in the entry and went through to the kitchen, where she filled a mug with fresh coffee and laced it liberally with cream and sugar. She glanced around the homey room with appreciation, eyeing her mother's colorful collection of patterned cups in a cupboard built just for the purpose of housing them.

She always felt like she was taking a trip back in time when she came here. It was comforting and nostalgic. She was glad, upon reflection, that they had not sold the family home and brought Erle and Alberta to live with them in their much smaller town house. Even though it might have been easier in some ways to keep track of their two loved ones, this solution, with Lucy in attendance, had worked out remarkably well.

'Morning,' she said, entering the cheery sunroom and bending to kiss her mother's forehead.

Alberta Norris sat comfortably ensconced on a wicker settee with brightly flowered cushions. Lucy sat nearby and the morning paper was spread out between them.

'Where's Erle?' Gail asked. The familiar little thrill of apprehension ran through her, even though his situation was so much better now. 'I have a couple of free hours this morning,' she added, 'and I thought I'd see if he'd like to take a walk.'

'He's in the playroom,' Lucy answered. 'I think he's working on a new magic trick. But I bet he'd love to go for a walk. Why don't you sit down and have your coffee first, then we'll see what he'd like to do.'

The three of them chattered over their coffee, talking about nothing in particular — local gossip, the new fancy store going in at the Seymour Mall, the price of gas . . . everyday nonsense that made no difference to anything, one way or another. Gail could feel the tension easing out of her body as they talked. She was glad she'd taken this time for herself this morning. It would make the work ahead easier.

Finally, she drained her cup and stood. 'I'll go see what Erle wants to do. If he'd rather stay here and show us his magic trick, I'm fine with that. I feel so much better, just getting away from the grind.'

Lucy smiled. 'All work and no play,' she said, 'can make Gail a very dull girl!'

They all laughed and Gail headed to Erle's new playroom, converted from her father's old office last year during the rest of the changes. She peeked in the door and watched a moment as her brother swished his magician's cape and waved a wand over a black silk top hat sitting in the middle of his crafts table.

'Abra-ca-dabra!' he shouted, squealing in triumph when a large flashy bouquet of flowers erupted from the hat.

'Hooray!' Gail called to him, stepping inside and clapping her hands. 'What a great trick! It's a new one, isn't it? I don't think I've seen that one before.'

'Gail!' The tall good-looking man in his early thirties turned toward her, his face breaking into a broad grin. 'You saw that, didn't you! Wasn't that a good trick?'

'Yes it was, Erle. I'm very proud of you. You're an amazing magician!'

She stepped forward, holding out her arms for his embrace. He planted a slobbery kiss on her cheek, then quickly broke away to run back across the room. 'And look, Gail! Look at this! Cousin Lucy got it for me at the store!' He held out a new coloring book featuring the Batman character. 'And crayons! She got me this big new thing of crayons.' He pointed to a red plastic barrel holding place of honor on the work table.

'That's wonderful, Erle. Lucy's a very nice person, isn't she?'

He nodded happily, gazing at his new treasures.

'I was wondering, Erle,' she went on, 'if you'd like to take a walk with me this morning. Just a short one, because I have to go to work later. How about it? Does that sound like a good idea?'

'Yes, oh yes, Gail! I was waiting and waiting and *waiting* the longest time ever for you to come! And I *want* to take a walk with you this morning. Yes, please!'

'Good. Do you have your walking shoes on? Yes, I see you do. We won't need coats because it's such a nice day. Let's go tell Mother and Lucy we're going.'

They finally got underway. After admonishments from Mother about not going too far, and Lucy insisting on fixing them a little pack loaded with snacks and small bottles of water, Gail and Erle set off down the driveway to the main road.

A little way along was a trailhead that led to a small pond. Often there were ducks and other wildlife there, and Gail could see how eager Erle was to get out and work his muscles. Because of his limitations, it was easy to forget he was physically a grown man with an adult's need for exercise.

They marched along companionably, stopping to look at various plants and flowers along the path; and at one point, to the surprise of them both, they spotted a mother deer and her fawn.

'Don't move or make a loud noise,' Gail cautioned Erle, who could hardly contain his excitement. 'You'll scare them away. Let's just watch them quietly for a little bit.'

'Oh, Gail,' he said in ecstasy. 'Aren't they the most beautiful things you've ever seen?'

'Yes,' she whispered back. 'Yes, they really are.'

Unaccountably, she felt a tear or two trickle down her cheek, just at the joy of it all. This beautiful summer day, her beloved brother happy and functioning so much better, and the sight of the animals feeding contentedly — all these things seemed like small miracles to her at this moment.

Eventually, in spite of their attempt to be quiet, the deer got skittish and decided to move on, melting back into the woods. Erle and Gail continued their meander to the little lake. This was a wildlife habitat, and along with the ducks and occasional geese, the pristine pool was well-stocked with fish. On the weekends, local families gathered here for fishing and picnics. But today, in the middle of the work week, it was completely deserted.

Gail found a picnic table in a shady spot and laid out a few of the snacks Lucy had fixed. Erle gulped down half of his water bottle and grabbed a handful of carrot sticks. 'Can I go over and see the ducks, Gail?' he said, nearly jumping up and down with anticipation.

'Yes, but don't get so far away I can't

see you, all right?'

He nodded happily and ran off down the side of the pond toward the area where the ducks usually gathered. 'Bye, Gail,' he called over his shoulder. It did not seem incongruous to her to see a grown man loping along, and hopping and skipping from time to time. But then he was her baby brother, and in her eyes he would always be age five, hopping, skipping and jumping along through life. She prayed she would live long enough to see him through.

Erle cavorted and played around the pool, feeding the several duck families bits of the crackers Lucy had packed (with just that possibility in mind, Gail thought with a smile). He and Gail walked a ways around the pool as far as they could go without getting into the marshes.

'All right, Erle, it's time to go,' she said at last, glancing at her watch. 'We have just enough time to get back home before I have to leave for work.'

In times past, he would have been uncooperative about leaving, and might even have thrown a tantrum. But today, even though she knew he would have liked to have stayed, he nodded in agreement. 'All right, Gail,' he said, smiling at her. 'I had a good time today. Thank you for bringing me.'

'Oh, you're more than welcome, honey,' she said, giving him a hug. 'You're a good boy, so it's easy to plan things like this for you. We'll do this again real soon, I promise.'

'Race you back!' he called, darting out ahead of her along the trail. 'Bet I can beat you back to the road.'

'All right,' she called after him. 'But wait for me at the road. *Don't go across it until I get there*, all right?' A cold finger of fear ran along her spine, but he turned back, a big smile on his face.

'Yes, *ma 'am*!' he called. 'I'll wait for you!'

She set out at a double click, panting, to try to keep up with him. It was less than a mile back to the road, but she wasn't used to putting this kind of a demand on her body. She was determined not to panic, however, and was relieved when she chugged over the final rise and saw him standing there at the side of the road, waiting for her as promised.

She stopped suddenly and veered behind a chunky pine next to the trail. Erle was standing there, all right, waiting for her as promised. But what she also saw gave her pause.

The road curved around to the right and disappeared over the top of a small hill. Sitting there right at the top, like some dark beast of prey, was a solid black sedan with tinted windows. Even at this distance she could hear the motor idling, almost like a purr or a growl — and a thin blue trail of smoke wafted skyward from the exhaust pipe.

Gail waited behind the tree, keeping an eye on Erle down at the roadside below her, and looking back to see whether the car would move forward, toward them.

Eventually, as if tiring of its game, the car pivoted, turned back in the other direction, and roared off into the morning. In a few minutes it was as if it had never been there — and all was silent again in the woods.

13

'I don't understand, Gail,' Connie said. 'What do you mean, 'it was as if the car was there waiting for us'?'

The four of them — Gail, Connie, Hugo and Jake — were gathered around the small round table in Gail's office to discuss what the two operatives had discovered at the ranch in Casa Grande.

'I can't explain it,' Gail said. 'I meant just what I said. When I got to the end of the trail break it was just sitting there at the top of the rise, idling. It really did feel like it was waiting for something. I know it sounds farfetched, but after how Hugo described the so-called 'devil car' at Rancho La Paz, it just gave me an eerie feeling, that's all.'

'And you actually hid behind a tree, just like Bolt did?' Jake glanced down at the precise notes he had taken at the interview with Henry Rowe.

'I guess so. It was just instinct, really. I

97

was scared to death that car was going to come down the hill at high speed and make for Erle. I thought maybe, if I kept out of sight, it wouldn't try that. I had the most incredible feeling that it — or the people in the car, I should say — knew exactly where I was. When I stayed behind the tree, they tired of their game and left.'

Connie shook his head, and Gail could see how frustrated he was. 'I'm sorry,' he said finally. 'I just don't buy that this was the same car as the one described in Arizona, or one sent by the same people. It's too much of a coincidence. And I don't believe in coincidence.'

'I don't either,' said Hugo. He had been taking in Gail's story and rumbling it around in his head, as he had a habit of doing, when he was worrying about a problem.

'If it's too much of a coincidence, then we have to look at it as a planned occurrence. And if it was planned around Bolt's disappearance, we must consider the possibility that this conspiracy goes much deeper than we think.'

'So you believe me?' Gail asked him, relieved that at least Hugo had not downplayed her story.

'Let's just say I believe that *you* believe what you saw. In my experience, even the slightest little detail can have a great deal of meaning.' He paused to take a sip from his water bottle. 'Just for the sake of argument — and mainly, just to humor me — let's put our minds together and see if we can come up with some sort of scenario that makes sense.'

For the next two hours the four spun various different theories about Gail's mysterious black car and the possibility it was somehow related to the reported sighting in Arizona. They tried to be as outlandish as they could, sometimes bordering on science fiction to pad their wild ideas. In the end they all agreed that, in order to make their theories work, there had to be some underlying motive for the mysterious black car and its odd appearances.

'Just how much is old Nino's estate worth, Gail?' asked Hugo at one point.

'That's hard to say,' she said. 'According to the appraisal, it might be in the tens of millions — and even might go as high as a billion. Nino was very close-mouthed about it all. Because some of the nature of the family business was, well, to put it discreetly, somewhat on the edge legally, there were various dummy corporations and offshore accounts, all of which have been set up to distract attention away from the true nature of the business's transactions.

'The supposed brothel in Nevada is just one such example. While it's perfectly legal in that county to conduct such an enterprise, the Del Monacos deemed it prudent to list it as simply a 'boarding house.' Needless to say, the income from that enterprise alone far exceeds what one might expect from a legitimate rental concern.'

She paused to clear her throat before continuing. 'And the whole estate is riddled with similar kinds of examples. Ralph claims that Nino talked to him extensively about all that during his final days. He says that Nino's overriding desire was to clear up all those anomalies and set the record straight. Then he hoped that Ralph would be able, gradually, to divest the family business of all things unseemly. His greatest desire was that his grandson would concentrate on positive, even altruistic, investments that his future progeny would be proud to own. I guess that qualifies as an underlying motive, if you will, for the reason the estate was devised the way it was.'

Connie had been jotting down notes as they spoke. He had not offered much in the way of further scenarios about the car, but he was beginning to get a fuller picture of just what was at stake here.

'So perhaps we could say,' he said, breaking his silence at last, 'as a premise, that a possible motive for scuttling Nino's estate plans could be that the rest of the family, Tommy and the others, are hell-bent on leaving matters just as they are. Once they got wind of the way their father and grandfather had stiffed them, I am assuming they, or some of them at least, want to leave things be, with them in control. Their huge motive is to keep the status quo.'

Hugo nodded. 'You're right, boss,' he said. 'I believe you have it exactly right. I think Tommy and his henchmen would stop at nothing to overturn Nino's will because they know it's in their best interests to leave things exactly as they are. In Ralph's hands everything would change, and they would lose all control over the operations they've grown to depend upon for all their money. Yes, I think that's where we have to concentrate.'

'So,' Gail said, 'you think they would stop at nothing in order to accomplish that goal?'

'Yes. I wouldn't put anything at all past them, including subverting Clinton Bolt for starters. What does Bolt get out of all this? Well, we know he was mighty interested in a big payday from Ralph. I think he might also be looking for reassurances from Tommy's bunch that there will be no repercussions on him if he cooperates with them. In other words, he may be playing both ends against the middle. I'm beginning to believe, more and more, that we've been duped — and duped thoroughly.'

'But what can we do about that now?' Jake interrupted 'How can we go about righting things after the horse is out of the barn, so to speak?'

'We've got to beat them at their own game,' said Gail. The rest of them looked at her. For the first time that day, she sounded very self-assured.

'And how do we accomplish that?' said Connie.

'Simple. We'll have to do a change-up.'

The others looked at her quizzically. 'What do you have in mind?' Connie said.

She could tell he was hoping she wasn't scheming something illegal and/or dangerous. 'Nothing elaborate — at least not just yet. But we've got to get smart about this.'

The longer they had talked, the angrier she had become. She was thoroughly convinced now that Clinton Bolt had played some sort of hoax on them. Why, she wasn't exactly sure. But she would have bet the farm it had something to do with money — a lot of it.

'First, I suggest we immediately file an amendment with the court to our witness list,' she said. 'We should add Bolt's name to it.'

Connie grunted. 'We didn't put his name on it at the time because we weren't completely sure we'd be using him,' he said. 'I don't exactly see the point in giving Tommy's lawyers a heads-up at this late date.'

'I'm not suggesting it to *assist* his lawyers, Connie. What I *am* suggesting is that we let Tommy know, in no uncertain terms, that we've got Bolt — and we intend to use him.'

'But that's just it, Gail,' interrupted Hugo. 'We *don't* have Bolt. And I don't see how in the world we're going to run him to cover before the trial. Are you suggesting we ask for a continuance? I doubt the court would go for that at this late date.'

'Look.' Gail brushed a wispy tendril from her damp forehead. 'I don't know whether or not we'll be able to find him. But my point is, *I'll bet Tommy doesn't know that, either*, unless they've got him under lock and key somewhere — and I doubt that, because of the story Henry Rowe told. They might not know where he is any more than we do. If they set up this scam, maybe we can turn the tables on them; make them sweat a little.'

'I see what you mean,' said Connie. 'If Tommy was behind this whole thing, it's possible Bolt is trying to scam him, too — hold us both up and go with whichever side is willing to pay him the most for his 'loyalty.' That makes as much sense as anything else.

'However, I still think we should hold off on Gail's suggestion for the time being. We still have time to amend the witness list before the trial. But let's wait and see if we might actually be able to find Bolt first.'

'Right, boss,' added Hugo. 'And now I'm wondering if there might be some clue to Bolt's whereabouts in that initial appraisal of the estate.'

'How do you mean?' Connie cocked an eyebrow at him. 'I don't see — '

'Well, how might Tommy offer to pay

Bolt off? Other than cash money, I mean. What would be an easy way to reward him for his silence?'

The others looked at him, waiting for the answer. Jake pounded a fist on the table. 'I know!' he said. 'I know exactly what Hugo's talking about.'

'Don't keep us in suspense, Jake,' said Connie with a smile. 'Share your epiphany, please.'

'We know that the bulk of the Del Monaco estate consists of various business holdings, buildings, hotels and the like. The most profitable ones are located in Nevada. But there are others scattered all over the place, including that hotel in Hong Kong . . . another in Miami . . . '

'Of course,' Gail breathed. 'Hugo, you're a genius! Connie, pull out that very first list of assets, the one listing all the buildings and businesses.'

'And? What am I looking for, guys?' Connie reached for the overstuffed folder next to him on the table.

'Anything . . . anything at all that remotely sounds like it could possibly be connected with Mexico.'

Connie grimaced. 'I feel like a fool. Right you are. I should have thought of it myself.' He pulled out a sheaf of papers and divided them with the others. 'That would be the easiest way for Tommy to pay off Bolt, if his challenge to the will is successful. He could choose, as part of his settlement, some business or building and deed it over to the guy. Makes sense Bolt would ask for something related to Mexico, if that's where he's decided to go to ground.'

They spent the next hour poring over the estate lists, jotting down possibilities as they went. At last, Gail glanced at her watch and stood up and stretched. 'Sorry all,' she said. 'I've got to leave you to it. I promised Mother I'd take them all to that buffet Erle likes over in Summit.' She bent and kissed Connie on the cheek. 'I won't be late, but I thought I'd extend the good time I had with Erle this morning.'

'Good until you were confronted by that devil car,' said Connie with a grin. 'Go ahead. We'll finish up here and choose some possibilities for follow-up tomorrow. How about it, Hugo? Will you both be free in the morning?'

'I've got a meeting about 11, but if you can be in by 9, I think we can make some decisions. I've thought of something else I need to do right away.'

They looked at him.

'I need to get back with my street informant as soon as possible. I should be able to get something out of him. He may not know the whole story, but I'll bet he has part of it at least.'

'Sounds good,' Gail said. 'All right then. We'll all meet back here tomorrow morning. Mr. Bolt may have a little surprise coming.'

14

Hector Lozano was in a hurry. When he checked the box at Kinko's that morning, the first thing that fell into his hands was a manila envelope containing a coded message from Bolt. All was going according to plan, according to the piano man; but everything now depended on himself, if they were to pull off this last big scam with any chance of success.

He scurried down the street as fast as his gimpy legs would take him, checking over his shoulder from time to time, worried about who might be following him. He had nothing to fear, he knew, from Ralph's defense team, especially his handler, Hugo. But Tommy? That was a different story altogether. Tommy Del Monaco had a short fuse, and once he figured out that Bolt was doing a reverse scam on him, there'd be all hell to pay. And he didn't want to get caught in the crossfire. He and Bolt went back a long way, but he'd throw that broken-down old piano player under the bus if he had to.

Just as he felt he was running out of steam, the red-and-blue neon sign 'The Uptowners Bar and Grill' flickered in front of him. Without hesitation, he pivoted straight toward the bar part of the building, ignoring the little notice stating the place was closed until 5 p.m.

In spite of the 'Closed' sign, the door swung in easily and Hector entered, relishing the sudden rush of dank beer-tinged air emanating from an ancient swamp cooler set into the back wall. '*Hola*,' he called out to no one in particular. 'It's me, Hector.'

After a moment or two, a figure peered in through a lighted doorway and moved toward him. 'That you, Hector?'

'*Si*, of course it is. Come on, Lou. I'm in a hurry.'

The barman ambled over and touched fingers with his visitor. 'How you been?' he said with a grin. 'Ain't seen you 'round lately. What you up to these days?'

Hector shrugged impatiently. 'You still maintain a drop-off for Tommy's *capo*?'

Lou looked at him curiously. 'You askin' for you, or some other dude?'

'For me, you ninny. What do you think? I got a 'special delivery' straight outta the horse's mouth for him. You collectin' or not?'

Lou swiped at an imaginary spot on the wooden bar with a grimy cloth. 'Sure, I'm collectin' for Tommy's *capo*. I was just joshin' with you.'

'Give me one of them *cervesas* while we're at it, will ya'? I'm parched.'

Hector sat down at the bar with a sigh. It was hot outside, and he'd been rushing around like crazy ever since he made the pick-up. 'I could use a cold one.'

'Sure.' Lou grabbed a glass and stuck it under the draft spigot. He placed the foaming brew on the bar in front of Hector and stared at him meaningfully. Reluctantly, Hector fished around in his pocket and tossed a couple of dollars at the barman.

'All right,' he said after taking a deep swig of the amber liquid, 'here's how this goes down. I've got a message for Tommy, and time is of the essence. *¿Comprendes?*'

'Where is this 'urgent' message?'

'Right here.' He patted the manila envelope. 'But I've got to have insurance on it.'

'I can get it in the next drop. Tommy's guy is due in here tomorrow afternoon. That soon enough for you?'

'It'll have to be, I guess.'

He took another deep drink then pushed the envelope toward Lou. 'I'll need the usual receipt,' he added. 'I trust you and all that, but I can't leave this one to chance.'

Lou nodded. He went to the back of the bar, reached behind the vintage cash register and pulled out a thick ledger book and receipt pad. Returning, he opened to a clean page and carefully transcribed all the identifying numbers on the packet into the ledger. Then he did the same with the receipt, signing it 'Louis Flores' with a flourish, and handed it to Hector.

'Thanks, Lou. I owe you one.'

Hector finished his beer and wiped the foam from his mouth.

'*De nada, amigo,*' the younger man

replied. 'You have a good day now, y' hear?'

'Same to you, buddy,' Hector said. 'Same to you.'

Leaving the precious packet in the barman's care, Hector got up from his stool and reluctantly headed out into the heat of the street.

Everything had been set in motion now. The next step would be a little trickier. He only hoped Bolt knew what the hell he was doing.

As he left the building and headed back towards town, he failed to notice a black sedan idling in a car park across the street. As he swung along, the car slowly pulled out of the lot and pulled in behind him. It kept its distance, however, with one or two cars as a buffer in between.

Hector, relieved that he had made his first drop successfully, relaxed his vigilance, and was none the wiser that someone else was aware of his big secret.

★   ★   ★

Hugo was exasperated. He'd tried contacting his street informant through all the normal channels, but the guy was not returning his calls.

'Maybe something's happened to him,' offered Jake, trying to be helpful.

'Don't say that,' Hugo said. 'The last thing in the world we need right now is to have that old coot do a runner on us. He's the key to this puzzle — or one of them, at least. I'll find that guy if I have to tear this whole town apart!'

Jake didn't reply. Hugo rarely lost his cool, and the young man didn't want to upset him any more than he had already. But Hugo was right. Their only contact with Clinton Bolt, really, had been Hugo's informant. Now that Bolt had disappeared, it was not a good sign that the only person who seemed to have any real relationship with him was also now on the missing list.

He hadn't told Gail and Connie yet, on the off chance he would pick up the trail soon. Right now he had every available operative checking out all the usual sources in the scummiest parts of town.

Something was bound to turn up soon. After all, the guy couldn't have just disappeared off the face of the earth overnight — or could he? Wasn't that exactly what *had* happened to Bolt?

15

Gail felt like she had spent so much time huddled over the Del Monaco account records that she was now hopelessly lost in a sea of numbers and misleading business entities.

'It's just like peeling back onion layers,' she complained to Connie, who was seated across the room at his computer. He was busy outlining their original defense plan, just in case their probes into the machinations of the Del Monaco organization failed to lead them to Bolt's hiding spot.

'Don't give up,' he urged. 'I think we're on the right track. Just remember, there are millions of dollars at stake here. We don't want it all to go to the wrong people, especially if they think they've put one over on us.'

'I just wish I knew more about this stuff,' Gail grumbled. 'I never liked dealing with numbers — even less do I enjoy delving into corporate jungles.'

Connie glanced at the time embedded in the lower right-hand corner of his computer screen. 'Come on. It's nearly 7 p.m. Let's give it another half an hour, then I'll take you to dinner.'

Gail nodded and turned over another leaf in the seemingly endless sheaf of papers listing the Del Monaco assets. Swiftly she skimmed down the left-hand column of names and numbers. It all seemed like a blur.

Then she spotted it.

'Connie!'

'What? Did you find something?'

'Come look at this. I don't know if it means anything or not, but it might be significant.'

Connie saved and got out of the file he had been reviewing. He picked up his notepad and pen and joined Gail at the conference table. 'Let me see.'

'Here.' She pointed to the entry that had caught her eye. 'What do you think?'

Connie nodded. 'I see what you mean. Let's see if we can find out more about this.'

About halfway down the page appeared an entry for 'Calitron Imports and Exports, L.L.C.' Next to it in parentheses was another notation in much smaller type: B de M. That was all, but the implication to both Connie and Gail was clear. It had to refer to the mighty Banco de Mexico, one of the most prestigious financial enterprises based in Mexico.

'Okay, what do we do now?' Gail asked. 'Can we just contact the bank and ask them for information about Calitron?'

Connie thought a minute. 'I know. We can ask them for the SWIFT Code assigned to Calitron. We'll say we need to make a payment to them via international transfer. We have all the information we need, but we don't know where to direct it. It's worth a try.'

'Yes, I see. We're not trying to take money *out* of the account. We're trying to put money *in*. It might work.'

'I'll send a message tonight to Banco de Mexico headquarters in Mexico City. With any luck, they won't question it and simply send us the SWIFT Code assigned to Calitron. If they comply, that may give us the location of the company's regional headquarters — and, hopefully, lead us to Bolt's hiding place.'

'I'm going to give Hugo a shout and get his take on this,' Gail said. 'He may be about ready to call it a day as well.'

An hour later, Connie and Gail were joined by Hugo at the bar in their favorite restaurant. As they made their way to a table, Hugo congratulated them on coming up with a possible link to Bolt's whereabouts. 'I just wish I could find my guy Hector now,' he said. 'I don't like the fact that he seems to have disappeared off the face of the planet.'

'Maybe he's joined Bolt in Mexico,' said Connie, looking over the evening's specials. 'After all, they may think we've given up on the case at this point. If Tommy succeeds at wresting control of the estate from Ralph, Bolt is probably in for a pretty big payday from him.'

'Yes, that's true,' Gail agreed. 'Still, there are too many unanswered questions to this puzzle to suit me. I wish now we hadn't sent Bolt out to Phoenix. It just made things easier for him when he decided to make his getaway.'

'I don't think it would have made any difference, Gail,' Hugo said. 'I suspect he had this whole thing figured out long before his pal contacted me. I think this caper has been in the works for a while.'

'Well I just hope, wherever he is, that Mr. Bolt is not as comfortable as we are here tonight.' Gail smiled. 'Good friends and good food. I'm feeling much better about our situation, gentlemen. Much better indeed!'

Later on that evening, an email was transferred from the Banco de Mexico headquarters in Mexico City to the computer in Conrad Osterlitz's private office in Cathcart. It contained a SWIFT Code number and a brief note, thanking Mr. Osterlitz for contacting them and expressing the bank's desire to facilitate his payment to their client's account.

'Now all we need to do is match up the SWIFT Code with the actual area it services and we should have a reasonable shot at pinpointing a possible location for Calitron,' said Connie.

'I'll put Hugo's bank specialist on it in the morning.'

'Then we have to decide if all this sleuthing is worth it,' Gail said.

'I don't know if it's worth it,' Connie said. 'But it irks me that Bolt thought he could play us like this.'

'And if he's *not* playing us?'

'If he's not playing us, Gail, I suspect Mr. Bolt is in a whole lot of trouble right about now. I don't know about you, but I'm not comfortable leaving this matter unsettled. I have a feeling we've just scratched the surface. I doubt we'll be allowed to just walk away from Bolt and his scheme, whatever it is. You're right — I think we have to play this out and hope it doesn't get nastier than it already is.'

Gail nodded. At heart she agreed with Connie. But she wished now that they had not been so eager to take Bolt up on his offer to testify against Tommy. It felt like they were in a no-win situation at this point. And given the choice, Gail would much rather be on the winning side.

16

Bolt made his way back across El Jardin and slowly headed for the warren of back streets that eventually would lead to his tiny *casita* in the poorest area of San Miguel.

He stopped every now and then, just like any other tourist, to take in the scenery. He gazed up and down the quaint cobblestone streets, looked into the open shops, and even paused to peruse a book or two from a table outside a red-walled colonial bookstore over-looked by La Parroquia de San Miguel Arcángel, the turreted sandstone master-piece that more resembled a fairytale castle than it did a local parish church.

He was feeling much calmer, serene almost, now that the crucial message had been sent on its way and the receipt was safely tucked away in his pocket. The die was cast. All he had to do was wait and see how it all played out. If he didn't hear back from Tommy with some sort of offer, he could either go back and testify for Ralph — or stay hidden here.

Lila had done a good job, as he had known she would. He had no doubt that after his veiled threat she would be too afraid to give him up — and it was unlikely she'd be questioned by anyone about his whereabouts in any case.

The barman at the cantina wouldn't be a problem either. *Mozo* had more than enough gritty legal issues of his own to ensure he wouldn't be contacting the authorities about any of Bolt's possible indiscretions.

No. All in all, things were moving along as smoothly as he could have hoped. He was relatively safe here, tucked away m his hidey-hole under the long-established alias. Not even Lila or the Hernández couple knew him as Clinton Bolt.

The only thing that kept nagging at the back of his brain was that one incident near the end of his time in Casa Grande. Something had told him to hang back and keep an eye on that long black sedan that had suddenly appeared on the horizon at the ranch.

He was no fool. He didn't believe for an instant that they wouldn't have come on in and tried to pick him up if they had wanted to. Maybe they weren't sure he was there — or maybe Tommy was just trying to send him a warning.

He shook his head. He was seeing phantoms now. And that would just mess him up if he let them get into his brain. He had to push on ahead with the plan on the assumption that he had caught Tommy unawares — and that the man had no clue where he was hiding.

As usual, he stood for a moment in the street outside the blue door and took in the sights, watchful for any unusual activity or strangers lingering about. Once he was certain all was clear, he followed the same procedure as before, entering and locking and bolting the outer door, before heading on into the living quarters.

He heaved a sigh of relief once he had closed and locked the double doors behind him. He never got over the feeling of satisfaction and security it gave him to know he was in a safe haven of his own making — which belonged to him alone.

He took out the receipt and looked it over again. Yes, everything was entered and signed for correctly. He smoothed it out, inserted it in a plastic bag and sealed it before heading to a corner of the room where he pulled back the threadbare carpet and used a screwdriver to pry up one of the wooden slats in the flooring.

Reaching down into the cavernous dark hole, Bolt pulled out a pale green tin box that had once held tea. Playful pastel kittens cavorted on its cover and he smiled at the conceit. He opened it and looked through the bits and pieces hidden inside: cash and specie of various denominations, a couple of passports and I.D.s in other names, and an old photograph or two.

He pulled these last items out and stared at them, misty-eyed, for a moment before returning them and the bagged receipt to the tin. He replaced the box in the hole in the floor, tamped down the slat and pulled the carpeting back over the spot, smoothing it out with his foot until all looked as it had before.

He fixed a light lunch and moved out to the patio to eat it. The dappled sun cast a few shadows across the brick pavers. The scent of the blossoms on the lemon tree was heady. It had been a good day today. He sat back and relaxed, opened a bottle of cervesa, and took a sip before beginning on the tapas, the plate of appetizers Luci had left for him.

All he had to do now was be patient and wait for the other shoe to drop. Then he would decide which side offered a better return.

A cloud rolled across the sky, shadowing his sunny spot. Before he knew it, fat drops of a tropical summer rain began splashing on the table, over and around him. He gathered up his lunch things quickly and made a dash for the door and cover.

He hoped the sudden rain was not an omen of things to come.

★ ★ ★

Later that afternoon the rain finally stopped but the clouds did not disperse, and the courtyard outside the French doors was full of shadowy puddles. The eaves kept up a steady drip ... drip ... drip, and the leaves of the trees played counterpoint.

Bolt felt restless. He wished he could venture out to one of the bright bars on the plaza, have a decent dinner and a few drinks and converse with the regulars. But that was not safe behavior and he knew it.

He played a few of his old songs on the ancient out-of-tune piano, but his heart wasn't in it. The days when he could noodle away for hours without growing bored were over now, and seemed pointless and vaguely dissatisfying. He supposed it was because he had lost his edge and knew his performing days were finished. Some players seemed to have the knack to go on forever, their gifts intact. He recognized he had thrown it all away, in honkytonks and third-rate hotel lounges, pitting his songs against tinkling glasses, inane conversation and booze-driven laughter.

The truth was, nobody wanted to hear

him play now. So there was no purpose in keeping his talent honed. No one cared. Least of all him.

The evening grew dark. He was thinking about getting ready for bed when a sudden rapping at the doors startled him. Damn! He knew he should have put the bar through the outer door. He relaxed when a familiar voice called to him from the darkened terrace:

'Señor . . . it's me, Miguel. I'm just checking to see if you need anything.'

Odd. It wasn't like the man to come here in the evening without being summoned. 'Just a minute. Let me unlock the door.' He dug around in his pocket and pulled out the key and moved to release the deadbolt.

The doors were flung open and Bolt stepped back. Miguel stared at him, a look of terror on his face. 'Sorry, Señor . . . so sorry.' Just behind him, a beefy paw on the smaller man's shoulder, a large black man loomed out of the darkness.

'Hola, Señor Shepherd,' came the gruff greeting. 'Long time, no see.'

'Dante,' Bolt said, using the other man's street name. 'What in the hell are *you* doing here?'

'Boss says you owe him, piano man. He says you owe him big time. He asked me to come remind you of your obligations. You run up a tab, comes a time you got to pay it off.'

'Let him go,' Bolt said, gesturing at the shivering Miguel. 'He's got nothin' to do with this, nothin' at all. He's just my yard guy. He's not going to do you any good in this situation, so *let him go*.' Bolt stared down the bigger man. It was important, he knew, not to show any fear or hesitation when dealing with the likes of Dante.

'Where are your manners?' Dante asked. 'Ain't you gonna ask me in?'

'Sure. You can come in,' Bolt said evenly. '*But let my man go first.*'

Dante took his hand off Miguel's shoulder and stood back. 'Bye-bye, little man,' he said mockingly as Miguel beat a quick retreat back through the courtyard toward the street entrance.

He pushed his way in and Bolt shut the

doors behind him. He opened the fridge. 'Cervesa?'

'Don't mind if I do,' Dante said, sitting down heavily in the mission chair, obviously the best seat in the house. 'So whatcha been up to these days? Playin' any gigs?'

'Nope,' Bolt said, taking a seat at one of the spindly wooden chairs at the table. 'I don't play anymore. Arthritis.' He held out his hands to display the long fingers with their gnarled knuckles.

'Well, ain't that a shame. I always took a fancy to your playin' back in the day.'

'Can't be helped, I guess. Price of growing old.'

There was a brief silence broken only by the sound of Dante taking another long slug from the amber bottle. He looked around the small room, taking in the second-hand furnishings and the threadbare carpet. 'Nice little place ya got here,' he said. 'Musta cost a pretty penny. How long you been here now? Can't quite remember when we first met up.'

'It's been a while,' Bolt said. He didn't offer any further comment, but waited to see what Dante would say. Inside, he was still taking in the fact that Dante had somehow gotten wind that he was here. He wondered if Lila had anything to do with it. He hoped the thug hadn't made any other connections, such as his association with the Del Monaco family and his Bolt alias. At least he had called him 'Shepherd.' Maybe his prior incarnation was still unknown to Dante and his boss. That would be one plus, at least.

But he couldn't count on it. He'd have to be damn careful now, he thought. One little slip and he'd lose the whole payday he was counting on. That was the problem when you did a change-up, he realized. You never knew when the wrong person might catch on.

17

Hector Lozano stopped and looked around before he entered the back alley leading to his crib. Something was making him uneasy, and the old man had been on the street too long to ignore such premonitions.

He paused, took out a cigarette from his hoard and lit it with a match. He inhaled too forcefully, and when the smoke hit his battered lungs he began to cough — a watery hacking that forced blobs of sputum up into the back of his throat. He spat into the street and threw the precious butt into the gutter with disgust. There it sputtered out in the noxious mix of drainage and debris left behind by a myriad of polluters. Cathcart's strained finances only allowed for regular street cleaning in the better parts of town.

He stood there for a bit, swaying and trying to shake the unsettled feeling. He squinted up and down the darkened street, attempting to make out any movement or suspicious forms in the shadows. Working street lights were not a priority in this area either.

At last he grunted and moved, as quickly as his cranky limbs would allow, across the sidewalk and down the alley into the inky blackness beyond. He was headed for a transom leading into a small basement storage area in a boarded-up warehouse that fronted on the busier street at the front of the block. Finding his landmark, he bent and pulled open the transom that had been left unlatched on the inside. He scooted through the slender opening on his backside, groping for makeshift steps with his feet. Once in the tiny cellar, he pulled the transom window toward him and latched it with a spare lynchpin he'd found in the tool area of the warehouse.

He turned into the room, feeling his way along a workbench fastened to the longest wall, until his seeking fingertips found what he was looking for — an oil-filled camping lantern. Reaching into his pocket once more, he pulled out the book of matches and carefully lit the lamp. The flickering flame cast back the shadows a bit and allowed him to get his bearings.

In a corner opposite the transom wall, an ancient grimy mattress sat, piled high with blankets scrounged from various sources and a few extra pieces of clothing. In addition to the lantern, the workbench held a package of sterno cooking cans, a few cans of beans and soup, a half-dozen water bottles, a box of wooden kitchen matches and an all-purpose can opener. He also owned one dented soup spoon and a battered tin cup.

These were the sum total of Hector Lozano's worldly possessions — the only items he needed to survive. He was truly blessed, he believed, that he had somehow discovered this tiny safe haven away from the hustle and bustle of Cathcart's city streets. In here he felt invisible and secure from prying eyes.

He sighed, pulled off his dank sweatshirt, tumbled on to the mattress and rolled up in the blankets. He had done a major job today, delivering that packet for Bolt. He hoped it would result in a big payday for him. Right now, however, he was bone-tired and looking forward to a little down time. He pulled out a half-full bottle of rotgut whiskey from under the blankets and took a swig. He hoped he'd be able to get some sleep tonight without pain or coughing.

The booze would help.

*   *   *

Hours later, as Hector dreamed anxious whiskey-fueled dreams of fleeing from nameless horrors, a scratching sound came from the hallway just outside his storage room. The warehouse had been vacant for years and, though boarded up, could be accessed from the main street with the proper tools.

Two hooded figures had sneaked into the cavernous space just after midnight. Working quickly and silently, they began pouring large cans of liquid in and around the office area and the hallway leading to Hector's hideaway. Satisfied with their work, they made their way back to the entrance; and, just before slipping out into the street again, one of them drenched a wadded-up rag at the end of a stick with the liquid, pulled out a cigarette lighter and set it ablaze. He threw it into the heart of the warehouse, then joined his companion on the sidewalk.

They watched a minute or two just to be sure the fire had taken hold, then dashed to their waiting car up the street. The area was deserted, and it would be a while before the smoke and flames would be noticed.

'So much for ol' Hector,' the fire-setter chortled to his companion. 'There ain't gonna be much left of *that* sucker to identify!'

18

Gail was not happy with herself. The phone had rung just as she was leaving her office, and when she answered, Mother's disembodied voice asked her if she had a few minutes to talk to Erle. He had a request he wanted to make of her.

Gail said yes, of course she had time for Erle. She waited until his breathy voice came on the line.

'Gail?'

'Yes, Erle? Mother says you wanted to talk to me.'

'Yes, Gail. Yes I do. I do want to talk to you. *Right now!*'

'All right, Erle. I'm here. You can talk to me. I'm listening.' She tried to keep the impatience out of her voice.

Connie had just texted her that he had retrieved the SWIFT Code for the bank servicing Calitron, the Del Monaco company that appeared to be located in Mexico, and that might give a clue to

Bolt's whereabouts. He and Hugo were going over the code now, hoping to isolate the three digits that would pinpoint the exact location of the Banco de Mexico branch where the company's headquarters was located. Gail had been about to head down the hall to Hugo's office when Mother called.

'Okay, Gail. Now, this is what I want.' Erle hiccupped and snuffled slightly. Gail wondered if he had been crying.

'Go ahead,' she urged.

'I want us to go on another walk again. *Please*, Gail. I'm *so* tired of my toys and my room . . . and Lucy has a *cold*, so she says she *can't* go right now. And Mother's too old and achy to go very far. Please, Gail. Would you take me for a walk again like the other day? Pretty please?'

Her heart sank. Not only was she too engrossed in this situation with the Del Monaco trial to even think of a casual outing, but she couldn't rid her mind of the image of that creepy black car idling its motor at the top of the hill near her mother's house.

'Erle . . . ' she began.

'*No!*' he cried. 'You're gonna say *no*, aren't you?'

Again she heard the snuffling sound that indicated another crying spell was on the way. 'Now Erle, calm down and let me explain.'

'Don't *want* you to 'splain.'

And the line went dead, indicating that Erle had broken the connection in a fit of anger. She only hoped this wouldn't lead to a full-out tantrum. He had made such progress over the past months. It would be a shame to see all the positive steps forward undone over this.

She was about to ring her mother back when another call preempted her. 'Yes?' she said.

'Just me,' said Connie. 'We're ready for you. Hugo's made some progress, and it's all very interesting. Can you come down?'

'On my way,' she said. But she was still regretting the outcome of her conversation with Erle. She would have to think up a special outing for him; one that didn't involve crossing the highway in front of the drive leading into the Norris estate. Something else entirely.

A change-up was what they needed. An alteration to their *modus operandi*.

'I think you're right. That's got to be it,' said Connie, running his finger along the column of identification codes Hugo had scrounged off the internet.

Hugo nodded. 'The first four characters are the Bank Code, the next two are the Country Code, the next two are the Location Code, and the last three are the Branch Code. Pretty simple, really. They're designed to make international money transfers easier and fail-safe. For our purposes, the two-character Location Code should tell us what we want to know. There's software that will allow us to do this.'

Gail shook her head. 'I'm glad you're on top of this. It's a little out of my comfort zone.'

'No problem,' Hugo said. 'It's just a matter of searching the codes until ours pops up.' He turned back to his laptop and touched a key.

'While we're waiting,' Gail said, turning to Connie, 'I've got to go out to Mother's again today. Erle's upset and I need to try and get him back on track again.'

'What happened?' Connie looked at her anxiously. 'Is everything all right? Do you need me to go with you?'

'No; I just need to talk to him. He wanted me to take him for another walk and . . . well, my response wasn't ideal and he was upset about it. I thought I'd see if he wanted to go to Seymour Park instead. He can do his exercises on the equipment there. Then we could stop and get an ice cream. He always likes that.'

'All right.' Connie smiled at her. 'Gail would probably like an ice cream, too!'

'Bingo!' Hugo hooted in triumph. 'Here it is. According to this, the Location Code attached to the SWIFT Code we were given appears to be the branch located in San Miguel de Allende.'

'San Miguel? That's some sort of an artists' and writers' colony, isn't it? What in the world would Bolt be doing there?' Gail looked from one man to the other.

'Well,' said Hugo, 'from what I've heard

of the place, it's a popular destination for expatriates of all sorts, including many Americans. I think it's located in the mountains somewhere outside of Mexico City. But I'll see what I can find out about it.' He rose and headed toward the door. 'Maybe now we can pinpoint where he might have gone over the border.'

'So you really think he did go to Mexico?' Connie asked. 'Won't it still be like looking for a needle in a haystack . . . finding him there, I mean? Even if we do know the city.'

'Difficult, yes. Impossible? I don't think so. Question is, do we still want to spend the time and effort on this? It's your call, boss.' He stood there in the doorway, waiting for direction.

Connie looked at Gail. 'I don't know. What do you think? Is it worth it to keep pursuing this, or should we just let it go?'

Gail didn't hesitate. 'The Del Monaco estate is worth millions. Ralph is our client, and we owe him the best defense possible. If we can find Bolt and convince him to return to testify against Tommy and his bunch, it might be worth every penny we spend on the effort. I say let's go for it.'

Connie turned to Hugo and gave him a thumbs-up. 'The real boss has spoken, Hugo. Do your darnedest.'

'You got it! I'll let you know what I find out about San Miguel de Allende, and just how difficult it might be to track down *Señor* Bolt — or whatever he's calling himself these days.'

★ ★ ★

Gail left the office in good spirits. If Hugo's instinct was correct, they might well be on the way to ferreting out Clinton Bolt's whereabouts. With further luck, they would convince him to come back to Cathcart and testify on Ralph's behalf at the upcoming trial.

She drove out to Long Hills, trying to focus on the beautiful summer weather and ignoring the nagging urge at the back of her brain to watch out for long black cars in the area. Traffic was light this early in the day, and soon she was pulling into the long drive leading to the Norris house. She parked at the front porch instead of under the carport at the side. Today she and Erle would drive to their destination instead of walking from the house.

She fitted her key into the lock, turned it and opened the door. 'Hello,' she called out. 'It's just me, Gail. Where is everyone?'

'Yay!' came a familiar shout. 'It's Gail! Hello, Gail!' Erle came chunking down the hall, his magician's cape swirling about him.

'Hi, Erle,' she said, giving him a hug. 'Are you ready for our outing?'

'Yes, oh yes, Gail. I am ready!' His innocent child-man's face was transformed with a radiant grin. 'Can we go now? Can we, please?'

'Where are Mother and Lucy? We have to let them know we're leaving so they won't worry about us, remember?'

'They're in the kitchen, Gail. I already told them we were going, so you don't have to.' He tried to stare her down but failed.

'No, Erle, *I* must tell them myself.

Otherwise they might think you left on your own. And you know that's not allowed.' She spoke quietly but firmly. This was a non-negotiable issue, and she intended to stick to their agreement. He must not leave the house on his own. After last year's debacle, which could have been disastrous for all of them, she was determined that he learn this one rule, if nothing else.

'All right,' he said, and turned to lead the way down the hall.

One small victory, she told herself. *One tiny little victory in this giant battle we are waging to save Erle.*

'Hi,' she said, following Erle into Alberta Norris's kitchen. The two ladies — her mother and her mother's cousin, Lucy — sat at the kitchen table. Lucy was peeling potatoes, and Alberta was cleaning stringbeans. Both looked up with smiles as Gail entered.

'Erle's been watching for you all morning,' said Lucy. 'He's been like a yo-yo, bouncing back and forth between the playroom and the front hall. He was so afraid he'd miss you when you came.'

Gail smiled back. 'No danger of that,' she said. 'I came just to see if he would like to go to Seymour Park with me for a while. We haven't been there in ages, and I'd like to see how he's coming along with his exercises.'

Seymour Park was a small green spot set aside near the bustling Seymour Mall. It had been dedicated by the Seymour family in memory of their deceased daughter, Vivian. One of its features was an exercise area, complete with posters explaining how to use the outdoor equipment to complete various routines. This was a favorite of Erle's, and Gail thought it was helpful to him in several ways. He could learn to follow simple instructions while getting a good physical workout. The other reason she had picked this particular spot for today's outing was its central city location and the likelihood that the area would not be completely deserted, even at this time of day.

'If it's all right with you two,' Gail said, 'we'll be on our way. We might make one more stop before coming back, but I don't expect we'll be too long.' She winked at the ladies, who understood she meant to take Erle to his favorite ice cream shop inside the mall for a treat after his workout. 'Tell them goodbye, Erle,' she added.

'Bye, Lucy. Bye, Mother,' he said before skipping back down the hall.

'Goodbye, Erle. Have a good time,' they called back.

Gail waved at them and dashed after Erle. He was over six feet tall and could outrun her easily. It was just one of the many challenges her brother could present if she wasn't vigilant enough while he was in her care.

★ ★ ★

'Now, do you remember how to do the exercises?'

Gail and Erle were standing at the beginning of a maze-like corridor leading to an inner yard set apart from the walled playground. There were ten separate stations, each featuring different types of metal equipment, and each marked with a large poster showing in detailed pictures exactly how to use it.

'Yes, Gail, I 'member. I can do it myself. You don't need to help me.' Without further ado, Erle ran eagerly up to the first poster, scanned it carefully, then turned his attention to the equipment.

'All right then,' she said. 'I'm going to go sit on that bench just outside the playground.' She gestured toward a seating area in the grass. 'Have fun!'

With a sigh of relief, she sat down and tried to relax. She tried to take her mind off the Del Monaco situation, but couldn't help coming back to it. Suddenly she had an idea. She pulled a small pad from her bag and jotted down a couple of notes. She knew without a doubt that both Connie and Hugo would be opposed to her proposal, but the more she thought about it the more convinced she was that it might be the perfect solution.

'How do, Ms. Brevard. Nice weather we're having, aren't we?'

Lost in thought, she was startled by the interruption, and even more alarmed when she recognized the man's voice. 'Mr. Del Monaco! What are you doing here?' she said.

'Tommy,' he said. 'Call me Tommy. What's formality among friends and acquaintances?'

'*Mr. Del Monaco*,' she said evenly. 'You know, I'm sure, that I'm not permitted to speak with you.'

'Oh, I'm not here to discuss anything *legal* with you, Gail . . . may I call you Gail?'

'It doesn't matter what you're here for. I *won't* speak with you, about anything.' She rose and hesitated, uncertain what to do with Erle nearby in the playground area. Glancing back, she could see two men standing next to *a long black car*. It seemed to her to be identical to the car she'd seen in front of her mother's place.

Tommy Del Monaco sat back on the bench. 'Just out for a drive this morning, Ms. Brevard. That's all. And there ain't no law against a citizen sitting in a public park on a nice summer day, is there?'

Gail turned back and resolutely entered the exercise yard. She strode toward Erle, about halfway through his routine. 'Erle,' she called, 'I want you to come now. We have to leave.'

'No, Gail!' He stopped what he was doing and gazed at her. She could see he was nearly in tears. 'You said I could do this! I'm not done yet!'

While facing him, she very carefully fingered the phone attached to her belt, hit a speed dial number and waited until she heard a distinct click that meant someone had picked up. Speaking loudly and clearly, she repeated: 'We *have* to leave Seymour Park *now*, Erle. I'm very sorry, but there's someone else here and we mustn't be here with that person. Why don't we go over to the ice cream shop in the mall and get a treat?'

Erle thought about that a moment, then got down from the curved pipe structure he'd been straddling. 'All right,' he said. 'Yes, I'd like to get ice cream. Can I have chocolate?'

'Yes, you can have chocolate. Now I want you to go find your jacket and wash your hands. I'll wait for you at the bench.'

Turning around, careful to leave the

phone line open, she headed back to the benches where Tommy Del Monaco sat watching and stopped in front of him.

'That the young Mr. Norris?' he said, gesturing toward the playground. 'Fine specimen of a fellow, I'd say. Tall, handsome, well-built. Any girl's dream.' He smiled broadly at his little joke. 'Of course,' he went on, 'it's a bloody shame about that . . . problem of his. Your dad musta been plenty disappointed when his son and heir turned out like that. And speaking of sons and heirs . . . ' he added.

'Mr. Del Monaco,' Gail said, speaking louder than necessary, 'I've told you I cannot have this conversation with you.'

'Was just gonna say,' he interrupted, 'that I sure do hope that brother of yours doesn't have some kind of accident out and about . . . given his predicament and all.'

'*Are you threatening me, Tommy Del Monaco?*' She spoke quite loudly now, hoping desperately that her phone call had been answered and that the person on the other end was acting on it.

'Why now, whyever would you think that, Ms. Brevard? Whyever would you think I might wish you harm?'

'Have you been following me?' Gail persisted. 'Because I thought I saw your car.' She gestured toward the sedan parked nearby with the two men lounging against it. 'I thought I saw it near my mother's place while Erle and I were walking.'

Just then, to her immense relief, two more cars pulled into the parking lot. The first, a Cathcart P.D. patrol car, with flashing red light atop, screeched to a halt and two officers jumped out and moved toward the men leaning against Tommy's car and asked them to identify themselves and explain what they were doing hanging around a children's playground in the middle of the day. The second car, Gail recognized immediately, belonged to Hugo Goldthwaite. It pulled alongside the patrol car and Hugo and Jake were soon at her side.

'We came as soon as I picked up your call and realized something was wrong,' Hugo said as Jake took up a protective stance between her and Tommy Del Monaco.

'What are you trying to do, Tommy?' Hugo said, turning to the older man. 'You know better than to pull an idiot stunt like this. What did you think was going to happen here?'

'Mr. Goldthwaite, I presume. And how is your illustrious father?'

Tommy was going to try and bluster it out, but he already knew that at least part of their conversation had been overheard and perhaps even taped. He sighed. This might possibly mean a trip to headquarters, if Gail decided to press charges against him for harassment. Such a bother. Still, anything to keep the other side off balance for a bit. Just until Ralph's defense team discovered the next big surprise he had planned for them.

*　*　*

A short while later, Gail, Hugo and Jake discussed the incident while Erle enjoyed his ice cream treat in the mall.

'I know I panicked and I probably

shouldn't have called you,' Gail said.

'No, you did the right thing,' Hugo said. 'Any time you're uncomfortable with a situation, never hesitate to call me or the authorities. Tommy was way out of line today. I overheard what he said about Erle — in fact, I taped it. He's going to regret that.'

'The way he was talking . . . I really started to think he was making a threat against us. And, Hugo? I'm absolutely positive that was the same car I saw out at Mother's. I'm not very good about car models, but it sure looked the same to me.'

'I don't doubt that you're right. I'm even wondering if those two goons made it out as far as Arizona last week, just to put a scare into Bolt at the ranch. Of course it could have been a local hire, or just a coincidence. We may never know. All the same, it's time we got serious about this.'

'So you think we might actually be in danger?'

'I wasn't going to bring this up so soon, Gail, but when you called, Jake and I were on our way to the morgue.'

'The morgue?'

'Yes. I got a call from one of my guys on staff there. He said they'd just brought in a John Doe. Burn victim, and so far unidentifiable.'

'And? What are you saying? Do you have an idea who it might be?'

'I still haven't been able to find my street informant, the man who told us about Bolt. This victim was found down in the warehouse district. According to my guy, there was accelerant all over the entrance to one of the back storage rooms, and an outside transom leading to the room from the alley had been blocked from the outside. The guy never had a chance.'

'And you think it might be your man?'

'Well, I hope not. But the fact that I haven't been able to turn him up through normal channels is puzzling. Ordinarily he's not that hard to find. He's always looking for cash, so he's usually pestering me all the time for a job. It's very unlike him to go into hiding.'

'Well, don't let me keep you. As soon as

Erle finishes up here, I'm going to take him home, then head back to the office and wait for Connie to get back from court.'

'I'll have one of my men keep an eye on your mother's house for a while. And tell Lucy if she sees or hears anything out of the ordinary to call 911 immediately. Better to have a false alarm than to wait too long.'

'Thanks, Hugo. And thank you also for coming to rescue me today. I wasn't quite sure how far Tommy would go. He's a creepy guy. I can see why Ralph wants nothing to do with him.'

'Just stay around people until you get out of the mall, and stay alert while you're driving home. You can't be too careful. You did the right thing today. Tommy and his goons will be kept busy with the cops for a while longer. But I don't believe for a minute that this will be the last of it.'

Hugo and Jake made their way out of the mall, glancing around to make sure there weren't any suspicious characters hanging around.

Gail sat watching Eric relishing the last of his hot fudge sundae. But her mind was not on ice cream.

19

Cathcart, with a population of just over 200,000, was the county seat of Carter County, and, with its outlying districts, was also the largest city in the county. The city boundaries, having been determined over time, were uneven, and produced a jigsaw-shaped puzzle to even the oldest of its citizens.

Legal issues within the city limits were enforced by the Cathcart City Police Department, and administered by the local district attorney's office answering to the town council and the mayor's office. All matters falling outside the city jurisdiction were upheld and maintained by the Carter County sheriff's office overseen by Sheriff Dick Williams and the county board of supervisors. The D.A. and the sheriff were both elected positions, and turf battles between the two entities were common and sometimes fierce.

The unidentified corpse uncovered in the smoldering ruins of the abandoned warehouse had become the source of just such a battle.

In the heat of the moment, the Cathcart City Fire Department had responded to the scene of the conflagration, as had the City Police during the following mop-up after the discovery of the body. Much to their combined chagrin, however, the Sheriff had immediately claimed responsibility for investigating the incident, since it was determined that the warehouse in question was just a tiptoe outside the city boundaries in an unincorporated pocket of the county.

D.A. Turner Redland, who had locked horns unsuccessfully with attorney Gail Brevard in prior cases, argued his point. 'It's a business district abutting up to the city, Dick,' he complained. 'We sent our guys out there in good faith and took responsibility for the whole bloody mess. I think it makes more sense for us to retain jurisdiction and handle it here.'

Turner Redland would be standing for

re-election in the fall, and a juicy homicide was just the ticket to get his name back in the news. Williams cleared his throat and considered a moment. 'Well, Turner, you may have a point there. I'll back off if you really want this mess on your hands.'

The truth was, Williams was only too glad to hand the bizarre death over to Redland. He had a vacation coming up, and the last thing he wanted was to get bogged down in some lurid murder case.

'Fine,' snapped Redland. 'We'll take control of the body here then. Thanks for your cooperation.' He was beginning to have second thoughts himself, but it was too late to back down now. Maybe it would be ruled an accidental death and be neatly solved without too much effort on his part.

So as a result, Hugo, with his inside connections with the city government, had been informed a day or so later about the unclaimed cadaver awaiting an autopsy at the city morgue. 'I'll be down there as soon as I can,' he had told his informant. 'Tell Doc I might have an idea about the identity.'

He hoped he was wrong, but it all fit. He knew his street informant had been holed up somewhere in that part of town. The fact that the man had not turned up in his usual haunts was suspicious. Hugo's never-failing instinct told him that the unidentified body was more than likely one Hector Lozano, his missing informant.

So after dealing with Gail's problem with Tommy, Hugo and Jake headed straight for the Cathcart city morgue and coroner's office, a large concrete structure surrounded by a small grove of fir trees and perched on a small hill just outside of the downtown area. It would have seemed idyllic if the purpose of the place wasn't considered.

They parked in the half-empty asphalt-paved lot, got out and headed toward the loading dock. Hugo pushed a button on the outer wall, and a few minutes later the large double doors rolled apart and a thin young man in scrubs peered out.

'Oh, it's you. Hiya, Hugo,' he said, opening up the doors further. 'C'mon in.

I kinda thought this one might interest you.'

'Hi Donnie,' Hugo said. 'This is my assistant, Jake. Hope it's all right for him to come in with me.'

'Sure, the more the merrier.' Donnie stood back and ushered the two detectives into the inner sanctum. A concrete hallway, wide enough to accommodate gurneys and transportation carts, led to another pair of stainless-steel doors in the bowels of the building. He motioned them to a small tram, climbed behind the driver's wheel and sped down the ramp to the main entry to the morgue. Once there, the three clambered off and made their way through the next set of double doors into an air-conditioned waiting room.

'Wait here a moment. Let me see if Doc can take you through.'

Hugo and Jake waited, grateful for the cool respite from the July heat.

'Hello, Hugo.' A tall, middle-aged man dressed in slacks and a lab coat stretched out his hand in greeting.

'Hi, Doc. Thanks for allowing us to

come in today. I realize how busy you are.'

'Nonsense. Glad to do it. If you can shed any light on this mystery it's well worth my time . . . and this is?' He looked at Jake in friendly interest.

'This is Dr. Bliss,' Hugo said to Jake. 'Better known to one and all as just plain 'Doc.' And,' he added, turning toward the younger man, 'this is my newest assistant, Jake Morrow. You may remember his father, Asa.'

'Of course! Glad to meet you, Jake. Your father is quite the man. Know him well.'

Doc Bliss offered his hand to Jake as well and shook it in earnest. 'Now,' he continued. 'Let's get down to business.'

He led them into an adjacent room set up as a lab and storage area. It was even cooler in this section, and by the time they had moved on to the final set of swinging doors, the temperature had dropped considerably.

Doc Bliss paused. 'Jake, have you ever done this before? Looked in on an autopsy, I mean?'

'I've seen dead people,' Jake said. 'But I've never been in a place like this before.'

'All I'm saying is, if you find you can't quite handle it, there's no shame in sayin' so.'

Jake paused. 'I understand. I *think* I'll be okay. But if I'm not, I'll just leave. Is that all right, Boss?' He looked at Hugo.

'That's more than all right. I don't like this much myself. So if you think you're getting a little green around the gills, don't hesitate to move away.'

'Yes, sir. I will.'

'All right then,' said Bliss. 'Here we go.'

The trio moved to a white enameled table in the center of the icy room, and Dr. Bliss carefully lifted a corner of the sheet covering the bundle there and pulled it away. Both Hugo and Jake couldn't help but gasp at the sight before their eyes.

The figure placed atop the table was in the shape of a human body, but it was just a vague resemblance now. From the top of what had been the head to the soles of the feet, there was nothing left but a charred mess. Clothing had melted into flesh, and both had congealed into what could only be described as barbequed meat left on the grill way too long.

The most riveting sight was what was left of the face. An elongated and gaping black hole sketched the mouth outlined by the jawbones hanging loose from their hinges. The nose was nothing but a cavernous space, and the eyes had completely melted away from their sockets. The result was a caricature of a face — a horrible cartoon one might see on a Saturday-morning children's show — and both men grimaced and turned away at the same time.

'Lord,' whispered Hugo. 'What a mess.'

Jake made a gurgling noise and stepped back toward the door.

'Go on, son,' said Doc Bliss. 'I don't blame you one little bit.'

'I'll be all right,' Jake said. 'I just need to take a minute.'

'Don't be a hero,' Hugo said. 'It's not necessary here.'

'No. I want to do this,' Jake insisted.

'All right,' Hugo said. 'Just don't get in the way.'

'I won't.'

Bliss looked at Hugo. 'Ready?'

Hugo nodded.

Taking a sharp scalpel, the doctor cut through the charred center of the torso, speaking into a recording unit as he went, ' . . . male, over the age of 50, approximately 5' 9" in height . . . weight, perhaps 170 lbs.'

Carefully he pried the rib cage apart and began removing the blackened organs and placing them on an adjacent gurney, describing each glob of cooked meat as best he could. Finally, he inspected the gaping mouth. Choosing a pick, he gently delved into the cavity, examining the crevice in great detail.

Hugo spoke up. 'Do you think you can find dental records?'

'Nope,' Bliss said. 'Something a helluva lot easier than that.'

Hugo looked at him.

Bliss smiled. 'Ever hear of DNA, m'boy? I found some nice pink tissue underneath all that char. All I need is a good swab, and if this guy's in the system, we'll know who he is soon enough.'

* ★ *

Gail sat quite still, willing herself not to respond too quickly.

'You there?' Hugo's disembodied voice came from the phone. 'I said the corpse found in the warehouse is my informant, Hector Lozano. Doc was able to match DNA from the body with Hector's records in the criminal justice system. The other thing,' he added, 'is that they're treating this as a homicide. Accelerant was found all over the place, and the transom he was using as access had been nailed shut. He was trapped in there, Gail. They burned him alive.'

'Oh my God,' Gail breathed.

'Are you all right?'

'I think so. But why would this have happened? And who would have done such a thing? Tommy?'

'I have no idea. But one thing is sure — Hector was just the messenger. Of course, we don't know yet if this is connected to Bolt's disappearance. But I don't like coincidences.'

'I don't either. Look, do you think

Bolt's still alive out there?'

'I think he saw this coming at the ranch in Arizona and went on the lam. He's a pretty smart guy. I think he knew exactly what was happening — and left before they got to him. My hunch tells me he's still alive and kicking somewhere. And my money's on San Miguel.'

'I've had this really crazy idea,' Gail said. 'But I'll need to talk it over with Connie first.'

'Where is he?'

'He's just coming in from court. Look. I'll bring him up to date on Hector and we'll make a decision on what to do next.'

'All right,' Hugo said. 'Just let me know when you want to meet. I'm mad as hell about what they did to that poor old cuss. He was perfectly harmless. That was no way for anyone to die.'

20

'No! Absolutely not!' Connie pushed back his chair and walked to the window. Looking down, he watched the nine-to-fivers stopping and going to the tune of the traffic lights spaced evenly along Main Street. Like a bunch of sheep, he thought, bleating their way toward the barn.

He turned back to Gail and began again in a quieter tone. 'I understand your reasoning. But do you really believe you're the best one to do this? That would be a horrendous journey — with no guarantee of success on the other end. We don't even know if this guy is really there or not. It would be like looking for a needle in a haystack. And even if you did find him, how are you going to convince him to give you a deposition?'

'Money, pure and simple. I think that's what he's after in this whole thing. And Ralph's already agreed to 'reward' him for his loyalty with a substantial stipend.

Let's not forget what's at stake here. Nino's estate could total in the billions by the time everything is added up. If Tommy is responsible for what happened to Hugo's informant, I don't want to see *him* ending up with the Del Monaco fortune.'

'Agreed. But wouldn't it be better just to send Hugo down there to see if he can find Bolt and convince him to return here for the trial?'

'That would be the best possible solution. But if Hugo finds him and he refuses to come back, for whatever reason, that pretty much leaves us where we started. We've got too much invested in Clinton Bolt to just let it all go now.'

Connie was silent for a moment, then said, 'I think it would be better if I went. This trial I'm on looks like it's going to stretch out forever. I can file a motion for continuance — or if that's denied, I can turn it over to one of the associates if necessary. I'm sick to death of the whole thing now, anyway.'

'You know that's not what you really want to do, Connie,' said Gail. 'You've

170

spent months preparing for this matter. You're not going to turn it all over to an associate at this late juncture. And a continuance is simply out of the question.

'No. We have at least two weeks before the Del Monaco trial. Hugo and I can fly in and out of Mexico in a matter of hours. He has some ideas about tracking down Bolt once we're in San Miguel. We can give it a week. If we're not successful by then, we'll come back and no harm done.'

'And if you run into any of Tommy's goons also looking for Bolt?'

'Hugo thinks that's unlikely. After all, presumably we're the only ones so far who have made the possible connection between Bolt and San Miguel. It's a long shot, I agree. But with millions at stake . . . '

Connie pounded his fist on the table. 'All right, damn it,' he said. 'I agree. But I want to talk to Hugo about all this and make sure we're all on the same page. I never like changing up a plan in the middle of things.'

But Gail was already on the phone.

'Hugo,' she said, 'get ready. Connie's agreed to the change of plans. Let's meet and set this thing in motion.'

★　★　★

Later that afternoon, Gail left their law offices and picked up her car in the adjacent parking lot. She spoke to the attendant, wishing him a good day, got in, adjusted her mirror and drove leisurely to the town house she shared with Connie at the other end of Main Street. Once there, she parked in her normal space, took her time getting out of the car, entered the building and checked the mail box assigned to them, removing a few letters and flyers. She moved to the elevators, selected her floor and rode up to their suite.

She entered, ignoring the fact that the alarm was not set, went to the bedroom, took out her smallest tote bag and filled it with a few necessary toiletries and an extra set of clothes. She then stripped down to her underwear and dressed in the clothing already laid out on the bed.

Slipping on a pair of loafers, she turned to the mirror. She removed most of her makeup and tied a scarf around her head, covering up her thick auburn hair.

'How's that?' she asked, turning to a woman seated in the corner of the bedroom.

'Looks pretty good, Gail. Here, let me . . . ' The woman came up behind her and tucked in a few tendrils of hair. 'I think that'll do just fine, with the glasses.'

Gail nodded. 'Thanks, Amy. Feel free to wear anything you like while you're here. I hope this isn't going to take too long.'

Amy laughed. 'Take as long as you like, Gail. This will be one of my easier assignments.'

Amy Cole was one of Hugo's operatives. She also had a build and coloring similar to Gail's. She had been given a key and preceded Gail into the building, wearing nondescript clothes, a scarf over her head and sunglasses.

Now the two women stood side by side, gazing into the mirror. 'Could be twins,' said Gail.

'At least that's what we hope.' Amy patted her on the shoulder. 'You be careful now. Don't take any unnecessary chances.'

'Thanks, Amy. And thanks so much for doing this. I know Hugo gave you a choice in the matter. You be careful, too. Especially if you see Tommy and his goons around.'

'Right. We'll *both* be careful.'

The two women hugged. Then Gail donned a pair of sunglasses with a fancy cat's-eye frame accented with one sequin above the left eye, picked up the small bag, and headed out the door. She made her way to the rear of the building and down the fire stairs to the back exit, then paused outside the door for a moment to get her bearings in the still-bright afternoon sunlight. Next she headed for a tan sedan idling near the alley.

She hopped in and looked over at the man in the driver's seat. He was wearing a tan suit as drab as his car, wire-rimmed glasses, and a pencil-thin dark mustache.

'Hello,' Gail said. 'You look about as interesting as I do. Ready for a change of scenery?'

21

Twenty minutes later, the tan car pulled up to the loading area at the Cathcart Airport. A woman got out of the passenger side, picked up a small carry-on, and walked leisurely to the entrance.

The car pulled slowly away from the curb and began the circle around to the long-term parking lot. None of this was unusual. A man was letting his wife off to get in line at the ticket counter while he parked, thus saving her the walk in from the lot.

As the woman entered the air-conditioned check-in area, she casually pulled away the scarf covering her auburn hair and tied it loosely about her neck. She removed the colorful sunglasses and tucked them into her bag. By the time she had circuited the half-empty back-and-forth maze meant to control larger crowds, she more closely resembled the picture in the ID she offered the counter clerk.

'Will you be checking your bag?'

'No. I'll carry it on.'

'I see your round-trip ticket to Houston is open-ended. Do you wish to reserve a return date at this point?'

'No. It's a family emergency. I don't know how long I'll need to stay.'

Quickly, the clerk completed her paperwork and handed Gail her boarding pass. 'Gate 12, through the concourse. This flight will be boarding in 45 minutes, so you'd better hurry to get through security.'

'Thank you,' Gail said.

As she made her way through the security check-point, she noticed a man just entering the area out of the corner of her eye. He was still wearing the rumpled tan suit, but he had lost the clip-on tie and glasses. Miraculously, the pencil-thin moustache was gone as well.

She did not acknowledge him. From this point forward they were strangers, and would sit in different sections of the plane for the two-hour flight to Houston, Texas.

As she strapped herself in preparatory for takeoff, she hoped Connie would be able to get the request for foreign deposition through to the Mexico City court system without difficulty. If they could find Bolt in San Miguel and talk him into giving them a deposition, they would still need to get him down to Mexico City to appear before the court there. It was supposedly an informal affair, often taken in an area where other business of the day was being conducted.

Their hope was that not too much attention would be paid to the details. Then all they had to do was convince the judge in Cathcart to accept the out-of-country deposition from a difficult witness.

Gail tried to rest for the remainder of the flight, but found her mind wandering back and forth. She was wondering, and not for the first time, if this wasn't a huge mistake.

Hugo, for his part, verified that Gail had made it on the plane, then hunkered down in his seat a few rows back and napped fitfully. He would need to be alert when they reached the next stage of their final destination. They would have to hike from their landing gate, through Houston's vast concourse, to the customs area and through that process without snags. Then there would be another round through ticketing and security and on to the departure gate for León before the final leg of their flight would begin.

Their actual time in the sky would not be long — two hours from Cathcart to Houston and another two hours from Houston to León. But the time they had allotted themselves for security and customs and just getting back and forth to their departure gates was tricky.

Customs itself was an unknown. Ever since the terrorist incidents in Paris and Brussels, and even last year's bloodshed in San Bernardino, flying had become more of an ordeal than a pleasure. The world of travel had definitely changed, and Hugo could only hope he and Gail would sail through inspection without too much difficulty or delay.

★   ★   ★

Meanwhile, in San Miguel, Clinton Bolt, aka Angus Shepherd, had managed to use every bit of charm and wit he still possessed to talk down Dante, the enforcer for the local money lender he owed.

'Man, you *know* I will pay back that loan — just as soon as I get this payday,' he said, opening up another bottle of beer for his guest.

'Look,' Dante said, 'I don't hold any hard feelings for you, Shepherd. But I got to keep the man happy, y' know? I can't afford to ignore orders. Now you know that.'

'I'm not asking you to do that. I'm just asking for a little bit of time, that's all. This payday is just about to go down, and it'll be a big one.'

'What kind of guarantee can you give me?'

Bolt hesitated. He didn't want to give the man any information that would put him or the operation in jeopardy. But he knew he had to give him something.

'All right. Here's what I'll do — and trust me, this is *all* I can do right at the moment . . . ' He proceeded to outline a story he hoped would satisfy the big man and his unhappy boss just long enough to get him through the next step in The Plan.

When he had finished, Dante took another big gulp, swished it around in his mouth, swallowed hard, and stood up. 'You screw with me,' he said, 'and you're dead. Simple as that. Noon tomorrow, near the bookstore in the square. No later.'

'I'll be there,' Bolt said.

Without further ado, Dante walked the few steps to the big double door, opened it and headed out into the night. A large bright yellow moon had risen directly over the little courtyard, almost as if on cue. Bolt followed his nemesis through the entryway to the outer door, opened it and let the big man out, then closed, locked and bolted it once more.

It would take every penny he still had in his account at the *banco*, but it would be worth it to get this goon off his back. He didn't like changing his plans in midstream like this, but it couldn't be helped. Now he would have to make the very best deal he could with Tommy — or Ralph, whichever one of them would prove to be most malleable. He only hoped Hector had received his message and managed to pass it along to both parties.

Everything depended on that.

22

By the time they reached their hotel in San Miguel, driving straight through from León in a rented car, Gail was ready to admit this whole affair might have been a big mistake.

Bone-tired, the two grabbed a quick bite at the hotel bar and made their way to their rooms. 'See you first thing in the morning,' Hugo said. 'Double-lock your door — and don't hesitate to call if anything doesn't seem right.'

'Okay. I just hope I can sleep tonight. I was too jumpy to doze on the plane.'

'Try to put everything out of your head. We'll get a fresh start in the morning. With any luck we'll get some sort of a handle on Bolt's whereabouts. If we can't find him in the next day or so, I suggest we give it up and head back. At least we'll have made the effort.'

Gail nodded, turned and headed gratefully into her room. She closed and locked the door, adding the double bolt as a precaution. A moment later she had trundled a straight chair from the desk in the room to the door and shoved it up under the handle. It wouldn't keep out anyone determined to enter, but it would make a lot of noise in the process.

She took a quick shower and sank wearily into bed. At least this place was clean and comfortable. Hugo said it was close to the center of town, which would make their initial searches easier.

As she drifted into sleep, a recurrent dream of a big black sedan hovering just at the horizon of the picturesque countryside they had driven through from León haunted her. She slept fitfully and finally, as dawn broke over San Miguel, she climbed out of bed and in to her clothes — ready, she hoped, for whatever the day would bring.

She buzzed Hugo, hoping she wouldn't wake him. But he picked up on the first ring. 'You up?' she asked him.

'Yes. I didn't sleep very well. Are you ready to get started?'

'As ready as I'll ever be, I guess. Meet

you at the coffee shop?'

'I'm on my way.'

Over a quick breakfast, Hugo began to plot out their day — but not before giving her his biggest news. 'I heard from Jake this morning. He's been querying customs at the various crossing points Bolt might have used to get to Mexico from the ranch in Arizona.' Most obvious was Nogales, but Hugo had dismissed that as being too close to the route heading straight south from the ranch at Casa Grande. 'I didn't think he'd want to cross that close to his last known sighting.'

'Are you still sure he actually got away? If Hector was taken out because of his connection to Bolt, can we be positive Bolt's still alive?'

'I think he's a lot smarter than poor old Hector. I think he had a pretty good idea he might be a target, and when he spotted that devil car at the ranch, he ran for it. And I think he would have taken a few precautions to make sure he got away free and clear.'

'So where do you think he might have crossed?'

184

Hugo smiled for the first time that morning and drank a bit of hot black coffee before replying. 'That's just it, Gail. We *know* where Bolt crossed. What's more, we know what name he's using.'

'Hugo! I don't know what to say. How is that possible?'

'Well, Jake and I put our heads together and looked at the maps. It seemed to us that the most logical places for Bolt to slip across the border — and the ones closest to San Miguel — were either Laredo, about a day's ride north of here by bus; or, even more likely, Brownsville.'

'Brownsville? But that's way down in the southern part of Texas.'

'That's right. But's also the closest route from the American border to San Miguel. That's what I'm trying to tell you, Gail. Bolt crossed the border at Brownsville earlier this week.'

'But how do you know that?'

'I have a contact there, a gal I've known for some years now. She runs the local travel agency in Brownsville and also provides information on customs for people passing through. She's authorized to issue passport and I.D. statements to American citizens who only plan to be down here for a short while.'

'And this woman remembered Bolt?'

'Jake asked just enough questions to trigger her memory about the guy. She said he was interesting enough to get her attention. Jake faxed her a copy of the photo we took of him and she responded right back. It was the same man — only he had darkened his hair, and he was using a different name.'

'Really! Was she able to give Jake the name?'

'She was. Said he was traveling as 'Angus Shepherd' and had recent documentation in that name. Of course phony papers are easy enough to come by, if you know who to ask. I suspect this isn't the first time he's done this.'

'Did she say where he was headed?'

'Yep, she sure did. Said he bought bus tickets through León to San Miguel de Allende. I suspect he's here right now.'

'So we were right with that wild guess, after all.'

'We sure were. Jake was getting ready

to talk to Connie about all this before he headed off to court this morning. This makes it even more likely you'll get that request for deposition approved by the court in Mexico City without too much difficulty.'

'This is great news, Hugo. I know Connie will be relieved. He thought we were on a wild goose chase. By the way, he texted me last night that he's staying out at Mother's while I'm gone. That way your team will only need to keep tabs on the one place.'

'Yes, Jake mentioned it this morning. I think that's a good plan, at least until we can take Tommy down.'

He frowned. Hugo was slow to anger, but he was still furious at the unnecessary and merciless killing of poor old Hector Lozano. Tommy Del Monaco was on his list now, and he didn't plan to rest until he had rid Cathcart of that particular sack of garbage.

23

'We'll be sorry to lose you as a customer, Mr. Shepherd,' the manager of the San Miguel branch of Banco de Mexico said. 'But I do hope your new location will be successful for you.'

'Thank you,' Angus Shepherd replied, tucking the envelope containing the cashier's check into his breast pocket. 'I've enjoyed my stay here, but now it's time to move on.' He stood, shook hands with the bank executive, and turned to leave.

Once out on the street, he heaved a sigh of relief. He'd left just enough in the account to pay the Hernández couple one more time, as well as any leftover utility bills that might show up. He still owned the *casita* outright, of course, but he would now have to shut off all the utilities and hope no squatters would make their way in before he could get back on his feet financially again and pick up where he'd left off. The check in his pocket would, hopefully, keep Dante's boss at bay until he could scrounge together the rest of what he owed.

That had been a big mistake, thinking he could escape the tentacles of the organization he'd borrowed a grubstake from a few years back. He'd hoped they wouldn't track him here from Mexico City. But he had been wrong, of course.

He sighed and glanced at the big clock affixed to the front of the building. 10:30 a.m. He still had a little time before meeting up with Dante. He decided to go back to the *cantina* where Lila worked. He wondered once more if she was the one who had given him up. He didn't think anyone else knew he was here — except *Mozo*, of course. The barman was a definite possibility.

Yes, he would head to the café and see if he could determine from the looks on their faces which of them might have told Dante he was back.

★ ★ ★

189

At the same time Clint Bolt was exiting the bank, Gail and Hugo were leaving the Rosewood Hotel. 'I'm intrigued by what you told me,' Gail said as the two headed down the cobblestone street toward the main plaza of the El Jardin section of town. 'Do you really think there's a possibility we might find him this way?'

'It's just a chance. I was going over all my notes last night, especially that first interview I had with him before I brought him in to meet you and Connie.'

'Is it merely a chance that we're taking, just coming here in the first place?' Gail steadied herself after nearly tripping on a loose stone in her path. 'I mean, this is a good-sized town,' she continued. 'It's really just a shot in the dark that we'll actually run into him wandering around like this.'

'I just have this hunch. Well, more than a hunch really. I guess you might call it an educated guess. I feel much better about all this after getting that confirmation from Jake about the sighting in Brownsville. At least we know we've got the right city.'

'So go on. You were saying he opened up quite a bit after you got talking with him.'

'Yes. He's really quite an interesting guy. There was one thing he mentioned that popped out at me when I was reviewing our conversation.'

They were nearing the plaza by now, and Gail couldn't help but marvel at the quaintness of the place. Shops and eateries, all housed in colonial-style buildings painted varying hues of red, orange and yellow, lined the street they were following toward a wide-open square in the distance.

In a way, she was glad they had come. She might never have seen all this otherwise. She could imagine returning here one day with Connie in the future, in that imaginary time when they had nothing to do — no trials to conduct, no research to undertake, and no tricky cases to solve.

'Go on,' she said, coming back to the topic at hand. 'What did he say, exactly, that you found so compelling?'

'He said that in addition to music, he

loved looking at old books. And here's the important part. He remarked that everywhere he went, whatever city, in whatever part of the world, he would hunt down old bookstores and browse through them, just looking at all the old books. He said he didn't often buy them; didn't have any place to keep them. But he just liked to look at them.'

'So you think he's doing the same thing here in San Miguel?'

'It's worth a shot. I asked the concierge back at the hotel this morning if he could recommend any old bookstores worth a visit.'

'And?'

'He said the most highly recommended bookstore in the city was Garrisons, just off the main plaza. He said you can't miss it. It's an old-style building painted bright red.'

'I've seen maybe a dozen buildings painted red.'

'Yes, but this one is right off the plaza. In any case, I've got the address. We can ask around once we're there.'

'Speaking of which, looks like we've

reached our goal.' Gail stopped as they entered a large open square. She caught her breath. 'What is *that*?'

'*That* is La Parroquia, the most famous site in San Miguel.'

Gail snapped a couple of shots with her iPhone. 'I wish I had my real camera with me,' she said. 'What an amazing sight!' The huge sandstone church sat on the south side of the square, its turrets and steeples reaching for the sky. The early-morning sun had tinted it pinkish-orange. Gail thought she had never seen a more imposing building.

Just then, Hugo grabbed her elbow and steered her to one side. 'Look!'

Gail strained to peer in the direction he indicated. At first she noticed nothing. But all of a sudden she saw them.

Clint Bolt was seated at a table in front of an outdoor café. His companion was a black man of imposing size. The two seemed to be involved in a heated discussion. Hugo and Gail stood there a moment, trying to decide their next move.

'You stay here,' Hugo said finally,

pointing to a secluded overhang. 'I'm going to go introduce myself; see how Bolt reacts.'

'Are you sure it's safe?' Gail asked anxiously. 'That man looks like he could be trouble. And they don't look like they're just having a friendly chit-chat.'

'I'll be careful. After all, there are quite a few people around. If it looks to you like there might be trouble, go ahead and call for help.'

'911?'

'Yes. That's the new national emergency number for Mexico since 2015. You can also dial 060 for local police, but you'll end up with 911.'

'And just stay put?'

'Yes.' He looked around. 'See, there's a little cantina right there. If you think you're being threatened, go in there and ask for help.'

'I'll be all right. Be careful.'

She watched as Hugo made his way across the square to where the two men were seated. She couldn't see Bolt's face as the P.I. went up to him, but she noticed that Hugo stopped well short of the table.

As Hugo approached, he rehearsed what he would say. This was obviously no chance meeting, and he would take his cue from Bolt's reaction. 'Good morning,' he said as he neared the pair. 'Nice day we're having, isn't it?'

Bolt looked up, curious at first, then in sudden apprehension when he realized who was addressing him. 'Hello,' he said evenly.

But Hugo couldn't help but notice that the older man's face paled beneath the weathered skin and day-old whiskers. All right, so the guy was scared. Hugo could see that, and he would act accordingly. He made the very quick decision *not* to use Bolt's name — or any name. If he was here incognito, it didn't serve any purpose for him to blow his witness's cover.

There was an uncomfortable moment of silence. 'Aren't you going to introduce me?' said Dante, his deep voice breaking the lapse.

'Of course . . . *Dick*.' Bolt nodded

toward the detective. 'I'd like you to meet an old — acquaintance of mine, goes by the name of Dante.' He had almost said 'friend,' but thought better of it.

'Dante.' Hugo stretched out his hand.

The big man touched it briefly and nodded. He sat there a moment as if deep in thought, then stretched his lanky legs and stood. 'I think we've concluded today's business, Mr. Shepherd,' Dante said, touching his shirt pocket where the cashier's check now resided. 'I *will* be in touch. Have a nice day, gentlemen.' So saying, he turned and strode away toward one of the side streets, thankfully not the one where Gail waited.

'So, 'Mr. Shepherd',' said Hugo, smiling at the other's bemusement, 'let's go someplace where we can have a quiet conversation, shall we?'

He nodded in Gail's direction, and she made her way over to join them. She had covered her auburn hair with the scarf again, and the sunglasses were back. With her drab clothing from the previous day's journey, she looked more like a local señora going about her daily chores than

196

an American tourist.

'Oh, my,' said Bolt/Shepherd as he watched the lawyer approach. 'This does change things a might.'

24

'So what shall we call you now?' Gail said. She had removed the sunglasses, but the scarf was still in place.

Gail, Hugo and the man they knew as Clinton Bolt sat in a booth in a little cantina just off the main plaza. Bolt had suggested the place and had led the way there. He appeared to be familiar with the manager, and had made his way to the table in the rear without waiting to be seated.

The older man gazed at her with a suggestion of a smile at the corner of his lips. But the blue eyes were cold as ice and reminded her of a reptile's stare.

'I'm known here as Angus Shepherd,' he said evenly. 'And for all intents and purposes, it would be best if you were to address me that way.'

'Very well,' she said. 'I guess you know why we're here.'

'I've got a pretty good notion.'

'Well,' she said, 'how about it? Would you be willing to drive down to Mexico City with us and give us a deposition there?'

'Deposition?'

'We would meet in front of an impartial representative of the Mexican court and witnesses of their selection. You would tell your story, just as we had agreed you would for the upcoming trial to settle the Del Monaco estate. We would take your deposition back to Cathcart and apply to the court there to allow it to be read into evidence.'

'They would allow that?'

'We're in the act of requesting it now. We would, of course, give evidence to the fact of your fleeing the United States and entering Mexico under an assumed name. That would support our request to take a deposition here, rather than try and extradite you back. It's complicated, but that's pretty much the way it works.'

Bolt was silent. The barman had come to take their orders. Hugo and Gail both ordered sodas, but he declined anything, waving the server away.

'What's in it for me?' he said.

'The same agreement that was made with you originally. Ralph has been very generous in offering to compensate you for your time and inconvenience. We paid all your expenses at the ranch in Arizona, including travel there. We'll pay you all your expenses for the trip to Mexico City.'

'No. I need more than that.' Bolt slammed his fist on the table. 'I've not only been 'inconvenienced,' as you put it. My damn life is now in danger. Too many people know about all this, including the man you met today. I'm treading a very fine line here . . . and I need to be sure I come out with a decent payday.'

Gail was silent and Hugo looked uncomfortable. 'How much are you talking about?' she said finally.

'Enough to make me whole again — isn't that the way you legal types put it? I've been damaged, through no fault of my own. Now I need to get back to where I was.'

'I'm not sure you can make a case for claiming that you've been damaged by

Ralph — or our firm for that matter,' said Gail. 'You came to us of your own free will, remember. We had no idea you even existed before.'

'There's something else you need to know,' Hugo interrupted. 'Something else has happened in the meantime that puts a whole other spin on this situation.'

'And what might that be?' Bolt sat back and crossed his arms in defiance. 'What other thing has happened you think might change my opinion?'

'Hector Lozano is dead.'

Bolt's face turned to ash. 'What did you say?'

'I said Hector Lozano is dead, and it was no accident. He was murdered in the foulest way. There's no doubt in my mind that he was the target of an assassination. What's more, there have been threats against Ms. Brevard and her family. You're not the only consideration here, 'Shepherd,' and it's time you owned up to *your* responsibility as well. I don't think we need to talk much further about 'compensation'.'

Bolt mulled all this over. Inside, he was

horrified. This had turned into a much worse scenario than he could have predicted. Not only was he still under threat from Dante and his boss for the rest of his unpaid debt, but there was no doubt in his mind now that Tommy had tired of all the game-playing and had decided to discourage his testimony — in any fashion he could.

Hector Lozano's death was a major blow to all of Bolt's plans. And he had no idea now if the old man had passed along both the messages he had sent.

'Did he talk to you at all? I mean, did you get any message at all from him before he died?' He directed his question to Hugo.

'None. In fact I tried to find him all last week, hoping he might be able to tell us where you were — or at least give us a clue.'

'So how *did* you find me?' Bolt was genuinely curious. It had given him quite a start when Hugo showed up at the table in the square that morning. Between that and Dante's unexpected appearance, Bolt's self-confidence had been completely shattered.

'Just a series of good guesses. You talked to people too much at the ranch. We did a bit of research about the Del Monaco holdings, which pointed us in the right direction. And finally, you left quite an impression on a certain lady in the travel facility at Brownsville.'

Bolt nodded. It all made sense. Hugo was a smart man, well-versed in his profession. Of course he would have put all those different things together. 'Still, that was a mighty good piece of detectin',' Bolt said grudgingly. 'I have to take my hat off to you. Not many would have come up with the exact spot at the right time.'

He laughed, openly this time. The joke had been on him. But now it was time to pay the piper. He made a quick decision. 'Take me back with you,' he said. 'I'm at risk on my own now. I see that. If you're willing, I'd like to go back to Cathcart. And I'll testify for Ralph without any further compensation than has already been offered. I'm too old and too tired to keep looking over my shoulder like this.'

'Go back with us?' Hugo said. 'But what about your I.D.? Would you go back as Shepherd or Bolt? I don't know . . . we hadn't planned on this.' He looked over at Gail, who was thinking hard.

'Do you still have the passport from Brownsville?' she asked.

Bolt nodded.

'All right then, we'll do it,' she decided. 'Hugo, you start figuring out what will be our best mode of travel. We'll need to settle up at the hotel and return the car.'

'No.' Hugo had been thinking hard also. 'I think we should keep the car and start driving back to the border this afternoon. The sooner we get out of here the better, and I think driving will keep us under the radar — for a while, at least.' He turned to Bolt. 'Do you need to pick up anything from where you're staying?'

'No, I've got my paperwork with me.' He slapped his breast pocket, where just a short while ago the cashier's check containing most of what remained of his life savings had also resided. 'I've finished my business here. I'm ready to go.'

'All right,' Hugo said. 'Let's grab a cab

204

back to the hotel. We'll settle up there and — '

'I don't even need to get anything out of my room,' Gail added. 'I've got everything right here in my bag.'

'Me either. Nothing there I don't mind losing. Okay then, we'll settle up at the desk, go get the car out of the lot and head out.' He placed a few bills on the table and rose, tossing back what was left of his cold drink.

Bolt followed Gail and Hugo out of the cantina with mixed emotions. It was amazing how much one's life could change in just a few moments.

25

Connie was frantic. He had heard nothing in the twenty-four hours since the last scant text message he had received from Gail. All she had said was 'plns hve chnged . . . cu soon.' Then silence.

Jake had heard nothing further from Hugo, either. 'He just said to 'keep watching the skies', whatever that's supposed to mean.'

'They must be coming in by plane. Well, keep monitoring the airport. That's all we can do.'

Connie had crafted the best legal argument he could for permission to take Bolt's deposition at the court in Mexico City. He fired it off with fingers crossed and prepared follow-up arguments to present if they turned down the first request. In the meantime, and at great surprise to him, he won the case he was trying handily. He cursed himself heartily for not following his better instincts and insisting on going on this crazy chase with Gail. It had been unnecessary for him to stay behind just to try this civil suit.

He had been staying at the Norris house and was under constant pressure to calm fears there about Gail's whereabouts and why it was necessary for one of Hugo's men to be stationed at the house around the clock.

'It's just a precaution,' he had assured Lucy that very morning. 'This case is a tricky one. Gail is with Hugo, so I'm sure she's safe,' he lied. 'And we just don't want anyone trying to harass any of you until everything has been settled.'

Lucy had just looked at him. She was skeptical by nature, and nothing Connie said made much sense to her. 'All right,' she said, clearing away the breakfast things. 'I'll be sure Erle stays in the house or the walled garden just outside. I've promised him we'll all go on a picnic when Gail gets back.' She looked at Connie. 'Now, just between you and me and the gatepost,' she added, 'do you have any idea when that might be?'

He shrugged. 'The last message from

Gail indicated they might be coming back sooner than they thought. But I can't say when that is exactly.'

'Uh-huh. So what you're *really* saying is you have no idea where she is or when she'll make it back.' She clattered the dishes in the sink and slammed a few cupboard doors for emphasis.

'I'm sorry, Lucy,' he said. 'I'm just as concerned as you are. But that's not going to do her any good, and it's not going to bring her home any sooner.'

'I'm sorry too, Connie,' she said, wiping a tear from her eye. 'I'm trying not to worry, but I can't help it.'

'Me either,' he admitted.

* * *

The rental car bumped along the road leading out of San Miguel on the way north to Nuevo Laredo and the border. They had decided to present themselves as a couple in a rented car with a driver. Hugo had steered Bolt into the men's room at the hotel and he had emerged with his dark hair slicked back, the tiny ponytail tucked into a discreet knot, and wearing the tan jacket, nerdy glasses and clip-on necktie he had sported earlier. The fake hairline moustache graced his upper lip.

Gail had covered her hair again with the scarf and was wearing the fancy sunglasses. Hugo had buttoned his shirt to the neck and somehow managed to lift a chauffer's cap sitting on the concierge table in the hotel lobby. They all looked quite respectable — nothing more than a couple of well-to-do American tourists being driven through the scenic mountains in style by their competent tour guide.

They were following almost the exact same route as Lila had a few days earlier, Bolt thought, looking out at the countryside whipping past the four-lane highway. The scenery reminded him of days spent long ago on the road in California — desert-like vistas of yucca and occasional green farm fields with purplish mountains off in the distance. The only difference was the occasional burro or horse grazing along the grassy strip in the center divider. Once they passed a herder guarding a small flock of sheep there. That was one sight you wouldn't see in southern California, at least not these days.

He would have enjoyed this journey if it didn't also mean the end of all his grandiose schemes. He recognized that he might never be able to come back here, and he had already decided to follow through and deed the *casita* to the Hernández family. It was the right thing to do, and he would probably have no more need of the place. His only hope now, he realized, was that Ralph would come through for him. There was no use in counting on Tommy, especially after Hector's demise. The man was vicious and dangerous. Bolt wanted nothing more to do with that side of the family.

He sighed and glanced over at Gail seated next to him in the back seat. She looked up and was startled to see tears gathering in his eyes.

'Hugo,' she said, 'see if there's someplace we can stop up ahead. I'd like to get out and stretch my legs a bit.'

'I think there's a Pemex a few miles further. I'll fill up and you can get out and walk around a bit. There are probably restrooms there.'

Pemex was the shortened name for Petroleos Mexicanos, the state-owned petroleum company that operated gas stations all throughout the region.

'Any idea how much longer to the border?'

They had been on the road from San Miguel now for about four hours. Gail had no idea how far they had come or how far they had yet to go.

'At least five hours, I think. But it'll all depend on traffic as we get closer to the border. If there's any food available, we should probably try to get something to eat, and coffee.'

'I'll check on that while you're getting the car filled. Angus can go with me.'

They had all agreed on using Bolt's alias, at least until they got across the border, since he would be using that passport.

Hugo said nothing further, but Gail assumed he was mulling over how safe she would be with the old guy. She had no qualms herself. She had sized him up and decided he was relatively harmless. And in this situation, at least, he was dependent on them, not the other way around.

True to his word, Hugo spotted a large Pemex facility just a few miles further up the road. He slowed and signaled, even though the traffic was light. He didn't want to take any chances on getting pulled over by the local constabulary. He pulled in to one of the open stanchions and stopped.

'Looks like there's a *taqueria*,' Gail said, pointing to a small hut with a large window propped open toward the street. 'Let's try there.'

Bolt followed her to the eatery and they decided on their order. Gail paid and together they carried the food back to the car. While Hugo finished filling the car, Bolt and Gail strolled over to a nearby grassy area and stood looking out at the mountains.

'I can see why you decided to come here,' she said. 'This is a beautiful place.'

'Well I won't be coming back now,' he

said. 'I'll have a price on my head from more than one source, and by now everyone in the world knows I'm here.'

'Don't sell yourself short,' she said. 'I can imagine you've had somewhat of a . . . demanding life. I understand you may have had to do things you really didn't want to do just to survive.'

He looked down. 'There's a lot of truth in that. I think I always just took the easiest route. Easy isn't always best.'

'But now you have a chance to make up for all that. If your testimony helps Ralph settle his grandfather's estate the way Nino *wanted* it settled, then you'll have done a lot to make up for any mistakes you've made.'

'Do you really think so?'

'Yes. I truly believe that. You're being very brave to do this. I understand your motives may not have been all that honorable. But in the end, the final result will be what counts.'

'I hope you're right,' he said. 'I just wish I could have continued on in that little haven I created for myself in San Miguel. No hope of that now, of course.'

'Don't be so sure. When this is all over, I think we can get you set up in some sort of witness protection program. You may not be able to go back to the same place you were staying, but there might be some sort of alternative that would suit you just as well. Don't give up hope, Mr. Bolt ... er, Shepherd. Things could change for the better. You just have to give them a chance.'

He looked out over the highway toward the mountains beyond. 'Why are you being so nice to me?'

'Look,' Gail said, 'my number one duty is to my client — in this case, Ralph Del Monaco. My next concern is my family. And I must tell you, we've been threatened by all this madness. My third priority is the firm and making sure we stay solvent — not only for our own benefit, but for all the people depending on us for their livelihoods. I'm not just 'being nice' to you. It serves all my purposes for you to be a cooperative and successful witness. And you can't do that if you're stressed out and worried about your own situation. It's very simple. I need you to be clear-headed and sure when you get on that stand. I'll do whatever I can to get you to that point. Besides,' she added with a smile, 'it doesn't cost me anything to be nice to you.'

26

When the little twin-engine commuter plane from Laredo touched down at the Cathcart Airport, Connie and Jake were waiting just outside the baggage area. As first Hugo, then Gail and Bolt straggled out of the concourse, blinking at the early-morning sunlight, Connie pushed forward.

'Am I glad to see you,' he said, wrapping Gail in his protective arms.

'I'm willing to bet you're not nearly as glad to see me as I am to see you,' she said. She leaned against him for a moment, then straightened up with a smile. 'Look who's with us!'

Connie shook hands with Bolt. 'Good job! Thank you for agreeing to return, Mr. Bolt. I understand what an ordeal this has been for you. I'm certain Ralph will be grateful for your cooperation.'

'I have to tell you,' the older man said, 'it was quite a trip. But here I am, and I'll do whatever I can now for the cause. Old Hector didn't deserve that kind of treatment, and I aim to see justice done.'

Hugo conferred briefly with Jake about logistics. Connie and Jake had brought separate cars, and it was decided that Hugo and Jake would take Bolt with them and get him settled under protective custody. Gail and Connie would go in his car to the Norris house.

'I'm looking forward to a long, hot shower and a good sleep in a comfortable bed,' Gail said as she and Connie headed out to the parking lot. He had offered to come around and pick her up, but she had no desire to be left alone at this juncture. She hadn't come all the way from Mexico to risk getting picked off in her hometown airport.

Later, in the sanctuary of her mother's home, she finally relaxed enough to begin to take stock of their new position with the upcoming trial. 'Bolt's a different person,' she told Connie. 'I believe he's had a complete change of heart, particularly after learning about Hector's death. I think he'll do his utmost now to put paid to Tommy Del Monaco and his goons — once and for all.'

'You did a great job,' Connie said. 'I had very low expectations for a successful outcome. Imagine, you and Hugo running in to Bolt like that in the middle of that square! It was just an incredible coincidence!'

'Not really,' Gail said, stretching out her limbs, catlike, in pure comfort. 'Hugo really had done his homework. I think we would have found him eventually, even if he hadn't been right there that first morning.' She laughed. 'I think he was as surprised to see us as we were to see him. And that Dante character? I have no idea what *that* was all about, but I think Mr. Bolt was just as glad as we were to see the last of San Miguel. Now,' she added, 'time to get to work. I have a few surprises for the Del Monacos. They won't know what hit them when we're through.'

27

'Once more,' Gail said, pulling her notebook toward her. 'Let's go over that last bit one more time.'

Clinton Bolt sighed. He was exhausted. It felt like they had been at this for hours — which they had. 'No matter how many times we go over it, nothin's going to change,' he said.

'That may be true,' Connie said. 'But we can't afford any mistakes now. This is as much for your benefit as it is for ours.'

'Don't you believe me?'

'We believe everything you've told us. I have no idea in the world why you would ever make up such a story. But more to the point, the judge must believe you as well.'

'And you think there's a possibility he'll think I've made all this up.'

Bolt sat back in his chair in resignation. As many times as he had stretched the truth, this time *was* different. He felt like the boy who had cried wolf too many times and couldn't find anybody to believe him.

'It isn't just that,' Gail put in. 'You must know they're going to bring up your drinking habits, and the fact that you were in that storeroom trying to sleep one off. They'll be going for credibility, just as soon as they figure out what you're going to testify about.'

Bolt mulled things over. He was still the only one in the room who knew about the packet he had sent to Hector and what it had contained. He had no idea if Hector had actually gotten word to Tommy, although he knew for certain now that Gail and her people had never received the second half of the message. Poor old Hector didn't have the opportunity.

So should he tell them? It seemed to him less and less likely he could expect any big payoff from Tommy at this point. He suspected that was a good part of the reason for killing Hector — to let him know all bets were off.

Just as he was about to speak up, Jake

rushed into the conference room. 'Bad news!' he said.

'What's happened?' Connie stood up.

'The worst. Lucy's disappeared.'

'What?' Gail was horrified. 'What on earth has happened to her?'

'We don't know. She insisted on going out today to pick up some groceries, even though Gary offered to go for her. Said she had a bad case of cabin fever and wasn't going to sit around waiting for nothing to happen any longer.'

'Why didn't Gary go with her?' Connie asked.

'He was going to, but Lucy insisted on him staying with your mother and Erle. Nothing much *has* happened since you got back, so he decided to humor her.'

'Where's Hugo?'

'He's on it. I called him right away and he's gone out to the house immediately. Told me to come in and let you all know as soon as I could.'

Bolt sat silently, listening to the stir around him. Felt like *déjà vu* all over again, he thought. Somehow he had to put an end to this madness. 'I need to say something,' he announced. But the others were discussing the current crisis and ignored him. '*I need to say something*,' he repeated, this time a little louder. They all stopped and looked at him.

'Do you have anything of value to contribute?' Connie said. 'Otherwise, the whereabouts of Lucy takes precedence over everything else.'

'Do you know where the old School House is up on Oak Creek Road?' Bolt said.

'I do,' Gail spoke up. 'What about it? Do you think they might have taken her there?'

'All I know is that there was a little joke among the boys that anytime somebody gave them trouble, they were going to 'take 'em to school and learn them a thing or two' — at least that's what I overheard more than once.'

'What is that place, Gail?' asked Connie. Gail had grown up here, but he was relatively new to the area. 'Isn't Oak Creek Road out there in the foothills by those old apple orchards?'

'Yes. It's the original one-room school

house for that area. It's been closed down for years. It was designated as a National Historical Landmark some time ago. Occasionally there are ceremonies held there, but most of the time it's completely deserted.'

Jake was quickly texting this new information as they spoke. 'Hugo and Gary are on their way out there now,' he said. 'They've called the state police as backup. He said for us to stay here until they know more.'

Gail was trying to keep back the tears. 'Damn them,' she said. 'I'm going to get that monster if it's the last thing I do.'

The rest of them were quiet as they waited for further news from Hugo. But they all agreed with her. It was past time to take Tommy down.

She noticed Bolt was trying to get her attention. He tugged at her sleeve. 'What?'

He looked down, a little embarrassed. 'I have to use the . . . facilities,' he said.

'Oh, all right. Jake?' She turned to the young detective. 'Can you escort Mr. Bolt to the men's room?'

'Sure,' Jake said, getting out of his chair. He held out a hand to assist Bolt in rising.

Bolt stood and faltered a moment, trying to get his bearings. 'I'm sorry,' he said. 'I seem to be a bit woozy.'

'Take your time,' urged Jake, holding the older man's elbow to steady him.

Bolt stumbled forward, grabbing for Jake's arm. He fell heavily against the young man and struggled to regain his balance.

'Easy there,' said Jake. 'I've got you. Take your time.'

'Are you all right?' asked Gail. 'Should we call a doctor?'

'No, no, I'm fine,' Bolt insisted. 'Just sat too long, I think. Happens sometimes.' He reached into his pocket and pulled out a white handkerchief and mopped his brow, then looked toward the door. 'Can we go now?' he added. 'I really need to . . . '

Jake held out his arm for support and the two men made their way out into the hallway.

Gail stared after him anxiously. 'I hope

he's all right,' she said.

'I'm sure he's fine,' Connie reassured her. 'He's been under a lot of stress the past few days. He probably just needs to get some rest.' He turned back to his phone to monitor for word from Hugo about Lucy's whereabouts.

Jake returned a few minutes later. 'I left him in the men's room. I think he needed a little privacy. Any word yet from Hugo?'

'Nothing yet,' Gail said. 'I hope this isn't another wild goose chase.'

Connie sat back in his chair and thought for a moment. 'Do we know what market she was going to?'

'She likes the little one just a few blocks from the house,' Gail replied. 'You remember, the mom-and-pop store run by that Indian couple.'

'We should check there to see if they remember her coming in. Also, we need to start looking for her car. I'm surprised Hugo didn't think of that first.'

'Maybe he did and stopped there on their way out of town.'

They went on waiting impatiently. Jake got a soda out of the little fridge in the corner. 'Want anything?' he asked.

'No,' Gail and Connie answered in unison. Connie drummed his nails on the table. Gail looked at her notes again. Time passed.

Suddenly Gail stood up. 'Where's Bolt?' she said. Both Jake and Connie looked at her. 'How long's it been?'

'He's been in there fifteen minutes, at least,' said Jake, heading for the door. 'Let me check . . .'

He was back in a minute. 'He's gone!'

'*What?*' Gail and Connie exclaimed as they looked at each other in horror.

'Gone again? What is the matter with that man?' Connie began texting an urgent message to Hugo.

'Oh, no!' Jake gasped. 'My gun is gone, too . . . and so are my keys! He must have picked my pocket when he fell against me. He's got my car and he's armed!'

Gail couldn't believe her ears. 'Why on earth would he do that?'

Connie looked at her. 'What if that Old School House suggestion was just to throw us off? I'll bet he knows exactly where Lucy is — and I'll bet he's gone after her. He's going to try and rescue her and take Tommy out at the same time. All in the name of revenge for his old pal Hector! The old fool,' he added, shaking his head. 'He's more likely to get himself killed in the process. Come on — we've got to try and find him first!'

$$\star \quad \star \quad \star$$

Lucy struggled to keep her wits about her. It had been such a short time ago that she had left the house with no more on her mind than keeping the grocery list in her head. She had gotten up that morning determined to get out of the house.

'Gary,' she said to Hugo's operative, reading the morning paper and drinking coffee.

'Yes, ma'am?'

The man was polite enough, but he was *always* there. And Lucy had just about had her fill of the enforced confinement.

'I need to go to the market this morning, that little one just down the road. I'll be perfectly all right, and I won't be gone more than half an hour. I really think this whole thing has gone too far. After all, I don't know anything at all about this case Connie and Gail are involved with. I don't see how I could be in any possible danger from anyone.'

'Sorry. I've got my orders, ma'am,' Gary said. 'I think Hugo will be by a little later on. Why don't you just wait and maybe he can take you.'

'Fuss and nonsense! That's just a waste of everyone's time. No, I'm going — and I'm going on my own. You'll have to tie me up to stop me!'

'Now that's just silly, Miss Lucy. You know I'm not going to do any such thing.'

'I mean it, Gary. I'm going — and that's all there is to it!'

So Gary, against his better judgment — and hoping Hugo would never find out — stood back and let Lucy gather her purse and a sweater and head out to Alberta Norris's old Buick sitting in the driveway. She motored down the road toward the market. It was a beautiful day, and she felt relieved to be away from the confining four walls of the Norris home.

She loved Alberta and Erle dearly, but she needed a little time to herself once in a while. Just too bad she had to make the excuse of going to the store to accomplish her goal.

She had just gotten out of her car in the nearly deserted parking lot at the Good Buy Market when a disheveled man approached and asked her for change 'to make a phone call.' Since most people of his age, homeless or not, carried cell phones these days, she was at once suspicious.

'Sorry,' she said. 'I don't carry change of any kind. You'll have to ask someone else.'

Before she knew it, he had glanced around to be sure no one was watching, then grabbed her tightly and slapped an evil-smelling cloth over her mouth and nose. Caught off guard, she stumbled and nearly fell. Choking and wheezing, she felt her knees buckle under her and knew she was losing consciousness. The cloth must have been soaked in some sort of knockout concoction.

The last thing Lucy remembered

thinking as she slowly sank into blessed oblivion was: 'Damn it, Gary was right! I should have stayed home after all . . .'

28

Clinton Bolt walked nonchalantly past the receptionist in the waiting room. She was chatting with someone on the phone and paid no attention as he exited the outer door and disappeared into the elevator.

He left the building and made his way into the parking lot, where he began clicking the beeper attached to Jake's keys until he got an answering response from a dark sedan parked near the entrance. He unlocked the door, climbed in the driver's side and looked over the control panel, familiarizing himself with the layout.

He started the car and drove quickly to the driveway and pulled onto the street, taking care to use his signals and allow the other traffic the right of way. No point in pulling a silly maneuver and risk getting stopped by the police. He glanced into the rearview mirror as he headed up Main Street towards the outskirts of Cathcart.

Good! They still hadn't missed him. They were probably just now beginning to wonder why he was taking so long in the men's room. Perhaps at this very minute, Jake would be checking on him. With any luck, he would be well on his way by the time they started trying to track him.

As he drove, he rehearsed once more in his mind what he was now about to attempt. He had a pretty good idea where Tommy's goons had taken Lucy — certainly not out to the remote school house he had mentioned. No. She was much more likely being held not far from here, in the warehouse district, and not far from the building where Hector had met his end. He knew for a fact that there were several similar deserted structures scattered about that area that were favored for such activities. With any luck, he would find her in the one he had in mind. Finding his way in would be a cinch. He had watched Hector do it many a time.

Then it got tricky.

He didn't have it quite clear in his

mind just exactly how he was going to free Lucy. But he had Jake's gun, he had checked that it was fully loaded, and he had no qualms about facing up to any of those young punks Tommy kept around. They were all basically cowards. If he kept that reality in mind, he might actually have a chance of pulling this off.

His only concern was that Gail's relative would not be harmed during the attempt. He would have to be careful about his approach. He just hoped they would have left only one man to guard her. That would at least keep his chances even.

★   ★   ★

Connie had pulled the CRT video from the surveillance camera trained on the entrance to the building. Sure enough, there was Bolt, first exiting the building and walking towards the parking lot. A moment or two later, he pulled out of the driveway in Jake's car and turned right onto Main Street. Connie watched until the car was out of sight. It did not leave

Main Street, at least as far as he could see.

'Gail, you stay here in case anyone calls in. Jake and I will head out and see if we can spot him.'

'Are you sure you don't want me to go with you? I feel useless just hanging around here.'

'No. We need you here to coordinate things and field any messages. I'll keep in touch by texting. If we do spot him, or the car, I'll let you know immediately. But I want you to stay here. No telling what we'll run into.'

Gail nodded. A few days ago she had gone off to Mexico without his blessing, and in spite of his misgivings. She had learned her lesson and wasn't going to do that again. He was right; it was better she stayed here and waited for word.

'All right,' she said, kissing him. 'Please be careful. We have no idea what Bolt has in mind, or how desperate he is right now. I can't believe he went so far as to take Jake's gun like that.'

'We'll be as careful as possible. Hugo's on his way back from the school house, and he's also notified the police as well. We'll have plenty of backup — and soon.'

She waved him on, then went to the big window looking down on the street. She watched as Connie's car exited the lot and turned right on Main Street. She continued watching until the car was so far away she had trouble distinguishing it from the constantly shifting traffic filling the street.

Reluctantly, she turned away and went back to the table, where she trained an eagle eye on her iPhone screen. She didn't want to miss any possible messages coming in from anyone.

*   *   *

Bang, bang!

Bolt found himself weaving merrily down a cobblestoned lane in Candyland, much like the cobblestone streets in his beloved San Miguel. He felt a vague sensation of heat — or *warmth*, really — somewhere near his left ribcage. He dismissed it as a petty nuisance and floated on, taking in all the miracles popping up around every turn in his new surroundings.

He wondered what had happened to the dank, dimly lit warehouse and the people he had come across there — the lone gunman guarding a middle-aged lady who must have been the missing Lucy. He shrugged, he thought, and moved on toward the sound of a trio playing nearby. It reminded him of the group he had once led so many years ago. They were doing 'Basin Street Blues' in the manner of the funeral bands in New Orleans that followed hearses to the cemetery.

He wondered who was dead.

The last thing he heard before he strapped himself in to blast off into outer space toward the Milky Way was a woman's voice saying, 'Hang on, Mr. Bolt. We're going to get you some help.'

He tried to thank her for concern about his space flight, but all he could see was the bright light of the rocket firing.

And then he didn't care anymore.

29

'Hear ye, hear ye.'

The Cathcart Hall of Justice was packed with observers and media, all waiting for a chance to watch the famous (or infamous) Del Monaco family come to terms with the conditions of the late Nino's last will and testament.

Gail and Connie were at the defendant's table with their client, Ralph Del Monaco. Behind them were arrayed several of the firm's associates and Hugo, Jake and several other advisors.

On the plaintiff's side, Ralph's uncle Tommaso Del Monaco and his sister Veronica Giuliani were flanked by several family lawyers. A few of Ralph's cousins were seated in the row behind them, but no other family members were present, including Tommy's remaining brother, Leónardo.

'Where's Lennie?' buzzed the watchers. 'I heard he's something of a recluse.

Lives down in Florida, I think,' one courthouse regular provided.

'You'd think he'd want to be here . . . at least to see what's going to happen to all that money the old man left.'

'Yeah, you'd think.'

The room was warned to quiet down as Judge Randall Craig took his seat. He was fairly new to this venue, and people craned their necks to get a good look at him. Gail and Connie had explained to Ralph that they would be trying the case before a judge.

'Why aren't we having a jury?' Ralph had asked. 'It seems like it would be easier to convince a dozen average joes rather than one legal person.'

'Trust or estate cases are normally not tried by jury,' Gail answered. 'Estate disputes can be complicated, and it's considered difficult for a jury made up of lay people to agree on what the person who made out the will really had in mind and do what's fair and just. Sometimes it's best to just rely on the legal expertise of the judge in such matters.'

'Okay,' Ralph said. 'I think I see your

point. You know best.'

And so here they were, about to start this case that had proven to be such a challenge.

As court was called to order, Gail hoped, and not for the first time, that they had thought of every possible angle. She knew they were well-prepared, but she had no idea how much the other side knew about their strategy and what kind of counters they might make.

'Ready?' asked Connie, glancing at Gail and Ralph.

'As ready as I'll ever be,' she replied with a smile.

'It's all in your hands,' said Ralph. 'My only hope is that Nino's wishes will prevail. None of the rest of it means a damn thing to me now.'

Howard Maddox, lead council of the highly touted Maddox Brothers legal juggernaut located upstate, rose to give his opening statement. He was a handsome silver-haired man of imposing stature dressed in a well-cut designer suit. Everything about him screamed class, money and privilege. He was often featured in television commercials advertising the firm's legal services.

Gail watched him carefully, trying to gauge how persuasive he would be during the trial. There were several other lawyers at the table, and they would likely take turns in presenting evidence and examining witnesses, depending on the areas of expertise involved. She and Connie would follow the same practice, but there were only two of them at Ralph's table.

Suddenly she felt apprehensive. Were they up to this challenge? And why were they so certain they would have the skills necessary to defeat Ralph's diabolical adversary? Maybe they should have called in more resources.

Connie noticed her unease and gave her hand a quick squeeze. 'Relax,' he whispered, as Maddox opened his brief to begin. 'We've got Tommy where we want him. Remember, right is on our side. We're going to wipe the floor with these goons.'

'Your honor,' Maddox began, 'it is my privilege to come before you to present the facts of this case. In June of last year,

Nino Del Monaco, my clients' father and grandfather, suffered a minor stroke. Up until that time, even though he was of advanced age, he had continued to oversee his family's interests with vigor and clarity.'

He paused and sipped some water before continuing. 'After a brief hospitalization during which he was examined thoroughly by the family's physician, Dr. Raymond Chan, he was pronounced well enough to return to his home under supervised care. My clients, who are the only living children of Mr. Del Monaco, were surprised and dismayed when his grandson, Ralph Del Monaco, the defendant in this matter, refused to allow them to have any part of the care of their father, and the planning for his future welfare and living situation.

'As time went by, it became more and more apparent that Nino Del Monaco was allowing his grandson to oversee the day-to-day business of the family, to the extent that he was buying and selling stocks and properties, purportedly at the direction of his grandfather. But again, there was no effort made to notify or include any of the other family members in these crucial decisions.

'Finally, towards the end of last year, Tommaso Del Monaco requested a meeting with Ralph and his father to discuss his concerns. Reluctantly, Ralph agreed, but it was obvious from the moment the meeting began that it was Ralph who was making all the decisions. Nino Del Monaco remained silent and uncommunicative through much of the conversation.

'Tommaso left this get-together deeply troubled, not only by his father's inability to convey his thoughts to his son, but by Ralph's total control of the situation.

'Sadly, Nino Del Monaco passed away shortly thereafter. The will he left, prepared by Ralph Del Monaco's attorneys, Brevard and Osterlitz — ' He nodded toward the defendant's table. ' — left all of his holdings, both monetary and real estate, to Ralph Del Monaco alone. Nino Del Monaco's two surviving sons, his daughter, and their families, were excluded from any mention in the will.

'It is this intentional exclusion of known valid heirs which is at the heart of the suit brought before you today. It is our contention that undue influence was brought to bear on an elderly man during his final days. We believe that Nino Del Monaco would not have knowingly excluded his closest living relatives, his own children, from any say in the disbursement of the monies and properties of his estate without undue influence and, sad to say, perhaps even duress.

'We trust that the court will view this matter as we do, and that justice will be served for Nino Del Monaco's rightful heirs, his sole remaining children and grandchildren. Thank you, your honor.' So saying, he bowed to the judge, the overhead lights bouncing nicely off his silvered hair, and stepped back to take his seat at the plaintiff's table once again.

'Mr. Osterlitz?' Judge Craig nodded to the defendant's table. 'Do you wish to make an opening statement?'

'Yes, your honor.' Connie rose and stepped to the front.

Gail tried to still her racing heart. She was suddenly aware of what a difference the outcome of this trial would make for them. The firm would be secure going forward far into the future. They would be able to offer many more benefits to their associates and employees. Mother, Erle and Lucy would be cared for, regardless of whatever happened to her and Connie.

Not only that. She knew without a doubt that Ralph Del Monaco would do the right thing by all concerned. He was already making plans for setting up a foundation in his grandfather's name that would benefit many people who were in need of assistance.

Yes, there would be far-reaching positive consequences for numerous recipients. Nino Del Monaco, through his grandson Ralph, would without a doubt pay it all forward.

Everything now depended on how well they presented their case. They had gone over it carefully, from this moment to the summation. Even with the surprise planned for Tommy, Gail knew full well that something could go wrong. She glanced at Ralph and smiled to reassure him. He looked a bit nervous, but he smiled in return. It would be all right.

'Your honor,' Connie said, 'I've listened to my esteemed colleague's opening argument with interest. While he's laid out the particulars of this case precisely and succinctly, I have a few additions and corrections I'd like to address on behalf of our client, Nino Del Monaco's grandson and heir, Ralph Del Monaco.' He gestured toward the table.

'Let me begin by saying that, while it is true that Nino Del Monaco suffered a slight stroke nearly a year ago, it is *not* true that the incident left him with a diminished mental capacity. Far from it. We will present evidence in the form of test documentation and statements from his team of doctors and therapists as well as others to demonstrate that, to the contrary of Mr. Maddox's statement, Nino Del Monaco remained in complete control of his faculties, in spite of his age and physical debilitation, up until the end of his life earlier this year.

'These statements will prove without a shadow of a doubt that Nino knew exactly what he was doing. He had a strong personality, and he spoke not only to his grandson Ralph about his final wishes, but to anyone else he came in contact with, including the members of our firm, as well as various representatives at his bank, his insurance agents, and others of the business community.

'We will be providing statements from all these people who had intimate contact with Nino Del Monaco during the final months of his life. They all swear, without reservation, that the patriarch of the Del Monaco family was adamant about what he wanted done with his estate and — even more importantly — why. We will also be supplying affidavits from *all* of Nino Del Monaco's physicians, therapists, and caretakers during that period who have stated that the man was neither senile nor unsure of what he wanted to accomplish — and just how that accomplishment was to take place.

'We have provided the statements and affidavits so described to both your honor and to Mr. Maddox. We will also bring to the stand a number of witnesses who'll testify both to the veracity of the multitude of statements gathered and to their own observations of the decedent and how he acted, both in the company of the defendant and when he was out of the defendant's presence.

'We believe that all of these statements combined will present the defense's argument in such a manner as to render further prosecution of this case both unnecessary and inappropriate. We hope the court will concur.' So saying, Connie bowed to Judge Craig and took his seat.

The judge glanced down at the paperwork in front of him. 'Is the plaintiff ready to proceed?'

'Yes, your honor.' Maddox's silver head bobbed in the direction of the bench.

'Very well, Mr. Maddox. Go ahead.'

A parade of minor witnesses followed, including a former housekeeper who had not been employed by Nino for at least five years before his final illness, the doctor who had treated Nino in the emergency room following his initial illness, an accountant who had been fired for incompetence a year or two earlier, a groundskeeper who thought his employer had been acting 'strangely' of late, and the like.

Gail took rapid notes of each witness and the crux of the statement made. Nothing so far was damning, but she was certain Maddox would be holding his key witnesses back until the end. She scribbled a note to Connie. 'Where's the surprise?'

He looked at her, raised a brow, and shrugged.

They took turns cross-examining each witness, even if there didn't seem to be much to say. They tried to discredit as much as possible the testimonies from the obviously disgruntled former employees. Gail went after Oscar Mayfield, the former accountant.

'Tell the court, Mr. Mayfield, under what circumstances you were relieved of your duties by Mr. Del Monaco?'

Mayfield squirmed in his seat and drew

out a snowy handkerchief to wipe his shiny brow. 'Would you repeat the question? My hearing isn't great,' he whined.

Gail spoke louder. 'I said, under what circumstances were you fired?'

Her recasting of the question did not escape the notice of the plaintiff's attorney. 'Objection!' called out Maddox, springing to his feet, silver mane rippling. 'Counsel is badgering the witness by characterizing his dismissal in an unflattering manner. There is no evidence to suggest that Mr. Mayfield left his position under a cloud.'

'Sustained,' said Judge Craig dryly. 'Rephrase your question, Ms. Brevard.'

'Thank you, your honor,' said Maddox huffily, regaining his seat.

'Yes, your honor.' Gail bobbed her head in deference before turning back to the hapless Mayfield. 'Mr. Mayfield, I ask you one more time. Will you describe for us the circumstances surrounding your dismissal from the Del Monaco account?'

Maddox was back on his feet. 'Your honor, she's asking the same question in a slightly different way. It's still leading — '

'Overruled,' grunted Judge Craig. He had tired of the game.

'Thank you, your honor,' Gail said. 'Mr. Mayfield? You may answer my question now.'

'Er . . .' Mayfield began, glancing over at Maddox, who was trying his best to look aloof and unconcerned. 'I guess me and Mr. Nino, we just didn't see eye to eye on things.'

'What things?' Gail pursued. This might be profitable.

'He didn't like some of the deductions I suggested. Said they were too . . . too *flimsy*, I think.'

'Flimsy? What do you mean, he thought the recommendations you made were 'flimsy'?'

'Well, I guess he was afraid . . . er . . . I think he was under the impression that some of them might not be . . . might not fly with the IRS, that's all.'

'He thought they 'might not fly with the IRS'? Why would that be, Mr. Mayfield, if the deductions you recommended were legitimate?'

250

'Objection!' Maddox jumped up again. 'There she goes again, making innuendos.'

'Your honor,' Gail said, 'I'm merely following up the line of questioning Mr. Mayfield himself opened by suggesting that something might not 'fly with the IRS.' I should be allowed a little leeway here.'

'Objection overruled.' Craig sounded a bit testy now. 'Let's get on with it, please, Mr. Maddox. I'm tired of arguing syntax with you.'

'Sorry, your honor.' Maddox sat back down with a huff and stared stonily at Gail as she took her time looking over her notes once more. Two could play this game.

She looked at Mayfield and shook her head. 'That's all, Mr. Mayfield. I think we can surmise why Mr. Del Monaco asked you to leave his employ.'

'Mr. Maddox?' the judge interposed before Maddox could once again object to Gail's remark. 'Any follow-up questions for this witness?'

Maddox merely asked Mayfield if, in

his professional judgment, Nino Del Monaco had a firm grasp on the accounting practices associated with his business.

'No, I would say not.' Mayfield felt on firmer ground now. 'At the time of my association with him, my opinion was that Mr. Del Monaco was fast slipping into dementia — and shortly would have been unable to conduct his own affairs properly.' So saying, he snapped his mouth shut and stared at Gail with satisfaction.

She thought briefly of objecting to the statement, but decided she had scored enough points at Mayfield's expense. Better to move on.

Next in the line of the Maddox firm's star witnesses was Agnes Carrey, Nino's former housekeeper. 'While employed at the Del Monaco house,' Maddox asked her, 'did you ever have cause to feel concern for Mr. Nino Del Monaco's ability to take care of his personal affairs?'

'Yes,' the middle-aged woman said, 'I most certainly did. There were times I wondered how in the world he got himself up, dressed and out of the house in the mornings.'

'And why was that?'

'Well, just for an example, he would often come wandering into the kitchen and ask the staff for their opinion on which tie he should wear. He didn't seem to be able to make a choice.'

Ralph tapped Gail and pointed at his notepad. She read what he had written there and nodded.

'Really?' Maddox said. 'Most interesting. Were there any other indications of problems your employer was having in making such simple choices?'

She thought a moment. 'I don't know if this counts, but there were times when he would start out the door, then come back because he had forgotten something — his keys, his cell phone, a file he intended to take with him, things like that.'

'Did he seem particularly bothered by these . . . memory lapses?'

'Hmm. No, not really. I think that's what seemed so odd about it. It didn't seem to bother him at all. He'd head out to the car, then first thing you know there he was back again, looking for something or other he had forgotten.'

'And you say this happened frequently?'

'Often enough that the staff joked about it a bit. You know, 'Here comes the old man, lookin' for his keys or the like. One of these days he'll forget to put his pants on . . . ''

There was a titter from the spectators, but an icy scowl from Judge Craig soon quieted them down.

'Thank you, Ms. Carrey. I think that gives us a good picture of the state of Mr. Del Monaco's mind.'

The woman started to rise to leave the stand, but Gail cautioned her: 'I'm sorry, Ms. Carrey. I have a few follow-up questions, if you don't mind.'

The housekeeper glanced at Maddox before sitting back down.

'Now,' Gail began, 'you say that one of the things you noticed about Nino Del Monaco was his habit of asking for guidance in his selection of a necktie?'

'Yes,' the woman said uncertainly. 'It

seemed odd to me that a man of his stature wouldn't be able to make an easy choice like that.'

'I wonder,' Gail went on, 'if were you aware that at a very early age, Mr. Del Monaco was diagnosed with colorblindness? That fact is well-documented in his family background and history. He even spoke about it on occasion, making fun of himself by saying that he couldn't even pick out his tie in the morning, much less fly an airplane.'

Agnes Carrey blinked in confusion. 'Why, I . . . no, I didn't know that about him.'

'Strange that you wouldn't know such an elementary fact about your employer. He apparently never made any attempt to hide that information.'

'Your honor!' Maddox jumped to his feet. 'Please instruct counsel to refrain from making editorial comments in the midst of her cross-examination!'

'Ms. Brevard,' Judge Craig sighed, 'limit your cross to questions, please.'

'Sorry, your honor,' she said. Turning back to Agnes Carrey, she went on: 'Now,

Ms. Carrey, you say that Mr. Del Monaco often forgot items when he left the house, and that this was a matter of great concern to you?'

'Yes. It just seemed odd to me, that's all.' Agnes Carrey was more cautious now, after the flub about Nino's being colorblind.

'I wonder. Were you aware that Nino Del Monaco had been under treatment for many years for OCD?'

'OC . . . ? Sorry, I'm not sure . . . '

'OCD. Obsessive-compulsive disorder. It's quite a common affliction, particularly among people of extremely high intellect. In Nino Del Monaco's case, it primarily manifested in a need to check things repeatedly before leaving the house. His condition was not a particularly debilitating one, simply an overly active compulsion to be certain he had everything he needed with him before he left home. Again, this was well-documented in his biographical information, and he never made any attempt to hide it. Also, for your information, it normally manifests at a young age and has nothing whatsoever to do with the aging process or onset of senility.' Gail paused and looked at the woman, who was flustered now, and near tears.

'I didn't know that. I really didn't. I can't imagine having a — a condition like that — and dealing with it every day as he did. I'm truly sorry we made fun of him. I don't think we would have had we known.'

'That's all right, Ms. Carrey. I'm sure he understood. And I'm sure you'll agree that Mr. Del Monaco was a very kind man. He would not have blamed you if he discovered you making fun of him. I think we're through with this witness, your honor.' She stepped back to the defense table.

'All right.' Judge Craig stood. 'I think it's time for a lunch break. Everyone back here at 2:00 p.m.'

★   ★   ★

The rest of the afternoon was taken up by the Maddox Brothers and their parade of disgruntled former employees of Nino

Del Monaco and the lone emergency-room physician who first treated him after the stroke incident.

'Please explain to us once again why you initially believed Mr. Del Monaco was suffering from a bad case of food poisoning.' Gail waved the hospital report in front of the reluctant witness during her cross-examination.

'By the time I examined him, the man had been waiting to be seen in the E.R. for at least half an hour. He came in complaining of nausea, and the admitting team prescribed a small dose of morphine just in case he was having a heart attack.'

'Morphine?' Gail's voice rose. 'Why on earth would they have prescribed morphine before a diagnosis of heart attack was confirmed?'

'Um . . .' The man was visibly sweating now as he scanned through his notes. 'Morphine is routinely used to treat chest pain associated with heart attacks. Mr. Del Monaco seemed to be in great discomfort . . .'

'Are you aware of recent studies that show use of morphine in such cases may result in an almost fifty percent increase in death?'

The young physician remained silent, glancing for assistance from Maddox.

Gail shuffled her papers and continued. 'Following the morphine dose, did Mr. Del Monaco's symptoms change in any way?'

'Yes. When I examined him, he was vomiting violently. Given his earlier complaint of nausea, I concluded that he might very well be experiencing a case of food poisoning. We began introducing anti-nausea medication. After a short while the vomiting ceased and he seemed somewhat improved.'

'Did you have access to his previous medical files? Isn't his regular physician on staff at the same hospital?'

'We felt, given Mr. Del Monaco's advanced age, that it was better to treat his situation as a full-fledged emergency and administer what aid we could before attempting to research his prior medical history.'

'Really? Did you know that highlighted in his medical records on file with both his primary physician and the hospital is the indication that Mr. Del Monaco was *allergic to morphine*? That any introduction of that narcotic to his system was almost certain to result in extreme vomiting and like symptoms, to the point of putting his life in danger?'

There was dead silence in the courtroom. The witness glanced down at his notes again. 'I didn't know that,' he finally managed. 'If that is the case, then . . . I am extremely sorry . . . '

'Yes, I'm sure you must be. Since you did not bother to check the man's history for something as simple as known allergies, you may have missed other key indications. I'm surprised Mr. Maddox is suggesting your testimony be relied upon for Mr. Del Monaco's mental acuity and capabilities during his final illness. Thank you, Doctor; that will be all.'

She turned and retook her seat. Connie gave her a discreet thumbs-up. This was the plaintiff's final witness for the day, and she had made short work of him.

They were doing well.

'How's everyone holding up?'

Connie and Gail had returned to the town house for the evening, and Connie had called Hugo to give him last-minute instructions about their order of witnesses before the next day's testimony began.

'We're doing fine, boss. We've all had dinner, and Jake's talked to everybody one more time about what to expect during cross-examination tomorrow. Anything further I need to know?'

'Not that I can think of right now,' Connie replied. 'But don't hesitate to call if any questions arise. I don't think we'll be getting much sleep tonight. Gail and I will be going over our strategy one more time.'

'Don't overthink it, boss. We're as prepared as we can be.'

'Thanks, Hugo. Have a good night.'

But Connie's nerves were on edge. Had they thought things through as much as they needed to? He was still angry about the threat to Lucy — and the aftermath to that confrontation.

'Everything okay?' Gail had changed into more comfortable clothes, but like Connie, she couldn't help worrying about how tomorrow would go. So much of their future depended on the outcome of this trial.

'Hugo says everyone's settled in, and Jake's been going over what to expect with them. Can't help feeling like we've missed something. I guess we'll just have to play it as it comes.'

Gail smiled. 'Now that doesn't sound like you. You're not into ad lib, that much I know.'

'I think the thing that worries me the most is that we really don't know what Maddox might have up his sleeve. I don't like surprises.'

'Except when the surprise is on our side, right?'

'Right. Except when the surprise is *our* surprise.'

30

Morning came too early. After a sleepless night of tossing and turning, playing everything over and over in her brain, Gail rose, started coffee and showered. Connie came out yawning as she was buttering toast.

'Want anything more substantial?' she asked, pouring a cup of coffee for him.

'No. If I eat anything now I'll be uncomfortable all morning. I can wait for lunch.'

'Did you sleep all right?'

'I think so. Although I had strange dreams.'

'Me, too. Someone was chasing me all over in a big black car.'

Connie grinned. 'Are you ready for your close-up?'

'I guess I'd better be.'

On the way to the Hall of Justice, Gail glanced again at their order of witnesses. 'Should we begin with the doctor and medical caretakers, or the housekeeper and other servants?'

'I thought we agreed we'd get the medical people out of the way first. Clarify Nino's physical situation and how it might have affected him mentally.'

'Yes, I think that would be best. But then, I'm wondering — should we bring in the housekeeper? Or his CPA and the bank people? Wouldn't they be more relevant?'

'I think we should stick to our original plan. I don't like the idea of changing things too much at this stage.'

'All right.' She drummed her nails on her bag. 'But what if . . . oh, never mind. Forget it. Let's stick with the plan.'

They made their way into the court-room, where they caught up with Hugo. 'Everybody here?' asked Connie anxiously.

'Jake's got everyone corralled out in the hall,' Hugo said. 'And — '

Just then, Ralph Del Monaco walked up. 'Good morning,' he said, shaking hands with the three colleagues. 'I sure hope we can come close to finishing up today. The suspense is killing me.'

'We've got a pretty full schedule today, Ralph,' Connie said. 'We'll try and get everyone in, but it all depends on how long cross-examination takes. It might very well go another day.'

Judge Craig made his entrance.

'All rise.' The bailiff waited until the justice took his seat. 'You may be seated.'

There was a brief flurry of activity as seats were regained, bags adjusted, and a few whispers were exchanged. The spectators looked about curiously, but the players were the same as yesterday. No obvious changes in the line-up at this juncture. The morning promised to be just as uneventful as yesterday had been. A few of the seasoned observers sighed and looked at each other in disappointment. This trial was not nearly as exciting as they had hoped it would be.

'Mr. Osterlitz,' said Judge Craig. Not a question really. It was the defense's turn at bat.

'Yes, your honor.'

Connie rose and called the first in a formidable parade of witnesses, including all the doctors, caretakers, servants, friends and colleagues of Nino Del Monaco the law firm of Osterlitz and Brevard could muster to support their contention that the deceased had been perfectly capable of attending to his own affairs and was under no duress or undue influence from his grandson, Ralph.

Maddox and company went after each and every witness, questioning, probing, and made every attempt possible to trip up the unwitting or ill-prepared. But the team had done their job well. No one cracked; no *faux pas* were made. The testimony went about as smoothly and effortlessly as Gail and Connie could have hoped.

Finally, just as they finished with their final supporting witnesses, Judge Craig glanced at the clock. 'Time to break for lunch,' he said. 'Everyone back here at two. Mr. Osterlitz?'

'Yes, your honor?' Connie stood.

'How many more witnesses do you anticipate you'll call?'

'Perhaps one or two,' Connie said. 'With any luck, we should complete our presentation this afternoon.'

'Good. Maybe we can get to summations tomorrow.' Randall Craig nodded, rose and made his way out of the courtroom. The spectators moved out as well, leaving the major players milling around at the front of the room, making their lunch plans and going over last-minute details.

'Are we ready — ' Gail started to say, when a booming voice interrupted her. A jovial Maddox blocked her way.

'Ms. Brevard, could I see you and your colleague for a moment before we head out?'

'Certainly, Mr. Maddox.' She gestured toward the now-empty defense table. Ralph had already left the room in the company of a few friends and supporters. 'What's on your mind, counselor?' she said, although she suspected she already knew. Connie joined them.

'I'm wondering if this might be as appropriate a time as any to bring up the possibility of a settlement between our clients? I think most of the witnesses on both sides have been vetted now. This case is a fairly simple one. I imagine we all, including Ralph, only want to see justice done. And after all, we are talking about Nino's *children* here, his flesh and blood. There's no point in being vindictive in these situations, I always say. It leaves bad blood among family members. Surely that's not what your client wants.'

Gail looked at Connie. 'Well you see, Mr. Maddox,' she said, 'Ralph would like to have his day in court. We have only one or two more witnesses. But we'd like to present our case as fully as we've planned. You do understand, I hope. I believe that our final presentation will set everything to rest — once and for all.'

Maddox frowned. 'But don't you agree, Ms. Brevard, that the longer this thing is spun out, the more resentment and acrimony will remain on both sides? After all, I'm sure Ralph doesn't want to permanently alienate his surviving family members — any more than they want to continue this painful feud.'

'You may be entirely correct, Mr. Maddox. But we'd still like to present our final case. If you remain committed to talking settlement at that point, we'll entertain the possibility. I *will* pass your request along to Ralph. But I'm more than certain he'll want to see this thing through, as Nino would have wanted.'

'Very well,' Maddox said, turning to leave. 'But you must know that the further along this goes, the less generous my clients are likely to be.'

'We'll take that risk,' Connie said, following Gail up the aisle toward the door.

* * *

As the courtroom began filling, Gail took her seat with mixed emotions. She was exhausted and looking forward to the completion of this part of the trial, which would clear the way for final summations and the judge's ruling. But the uncertainty of the outcome weighed heavily on her. Had they made the right decision about their presentation? And what if someone — Tommy or his goons, perhaps — chose to put their own spin on the final decision?

They all had to pass through the metal detector at the entrance to the building. All bags were searched. But there was always the remote possibility someone would manage to sneak through security with a hidden weapon. There had already been more than enough violence in this case, some of it affecting Gail's family. Would justice be served by pursuing this case? she wondered. Or would the family trauma, both Ralph's and hers, be intensified? She wished she had answers to these questions, but none came readily.

Connie reached over and squeezed her hand in support. He, of all people, understood her uncertainty and shared it.

She squeezed back and smiled at him. 'It's going to be all right,' she said. 'I believe everything will go smoothly.' She only hoped her positive outlook would see her through.

Judge Craig entered and the bailiff called for all to rise. The magistrate reviewed the file in front of him to refresh his memory of what had transpired earlier in the day.

'Mr. Osterlitz?'

'Yes, your honor,' Connie said, standing at attention.

'Are you ready to proceed? You said you had several more witnesses?'

'Yes, we're ready.' He looked down at his notes. 'The defense calls Hugo Goldthwaite to the stand.'

A little ripple of anticipation ran through the crowd. Maddox looked up sharply. Hugo's name had not been on the preliminary witness list. He started to rise to object, then thought better of it. May as well see where this was headed.

Hugo came in from the hall, where he had been awaiting his cue. He made his way to the front of the room, giving a brief nod to Gail as he passed the defense table. He was sworn and took his seat in the witness chair.

'Would you please give your name and occupation for the benefit of the court?' Connie said.

'My name is Hugo Goldthwaite, Jr. I am owner and proprietor of the Goldthwaite Detective Agency.'

'And what is your relationship to the firm of Osterlitz and Brevard?'

'I'm on permanent retainer by the firm for the purposes of assisting in gathering information on clients and others involved in the various cases they're handling. My offices are located adjacent to the firm's offices in the same building.'

'And in the course of your duties, have you had occasion in recent weeks to assist the firm in preparing for this case regarding their client, Ralph Del Monaco?'

'Yes, I have.' Hugo had testified many times in the past in such cases. He was well-versed in the procedure and was careful not to offer more information than necessary.

'And while pursuing your enquiries concerning this case, did certain unusual events transpire? Events that may have a bearing on the final outcome of this case?'

Maddox jumped to his feet. 'Your honor!' he shouted. 'This is outrageous! Counsel is changing all the parameters of this case by bringing in new and undisclosed information. I question whether any of this has any bearing at all on what we're trying to decide here.'

'Your honor,' Connie spoke up, 'these events most certainly *do* have a bearing on the case at hand, in significant ways. In fact, I don't see how a complete and fair verdict can be rendered without the information we're prepared to offer today.'

Judge Craig sighed. 'Approach,' he said. This was not going to end as smoothly as he had hoped.

Maddox and his assistant and Connie and Gail made their way to the bench.

'What's going on here?' Craig rasped at Connie. 'There'd better be a connection in all this.'

'There is, your honor,' Connie replied. 'But I must be allowed some leeway. We have two, maybe three more witnesses. You cannot render a comprehensive judgment on this case without hearing them out.'

'Your honor!' Maddox was livid. 'This is unconscionable! It's a fishing expedition, nothing less. I doubt if Goldthwaite, or any other witness they dredge up, will have anything material to offer to your decision.'

'I assure you, your honor' Connie repeated, 'you *must* hear these witnesses. Their testimony is vital to our defense.'

Randall Craig took a moment. He was not new to the process, and he often had a feel for the rightness or wrongness of a situation. He looked at Connie hard and made his decision. 'Overruled,' he said. 'We'll see where this leads. But I'm reminding you, Mr. Osterlitz, make your connection and make it quick.'

Everyone returned to their former places. Connie turned back to Hugo. 'I want to take you back to the week following the Fourth of July holiday weekend. You came to Ms. Brevard and me with a potential witness for this specific case. Do you recall the circumstances of that meeting, and will you elaborate on that for the court?'

'Yes. On the Monday following the holiday I received a phone call from a man I'll describe as a street informant of mine. I'd known him for some years, and he'd always been reliable in his dealings with me in the past. So I had no qualms about following up with him on this occasion.'

'And what was the nature of the information he offered you?'

'He said that someone he knew, a friend of sorts, had a story to tell, something specific to the Del Monaco lawsuit. I met with him and he introduced me to his friend, a man named Clinton Bolt.'

There was a gasp from the plaintiff's table. Tommy Del Monaco whispered urgently to Maddox. Veronica Giuliani looked confused.

'Order!' Judge Craig pounded his gavel. 'No more outbursts from the plaintiff!'

'Please continue,' Connie said to his witness.

'I talked to Bolt a bit, then decided you and Ms. Brevard needed to hear him out. I brought him back to the office and he told us his story in full.'

'How did his story coincide with the lawsuit being brought against Ralph Del Monaco by other members of the Del Monaco family?'

Before Hugo could answer, Maddox jumped up again. 'Hearsay,' he said. 'If this man's testimony is so valuable to the defense, why isn't he here to testify?'

'I'm glad you asked that, counselor,' Connie inserted smoothly. 'Before we could make the final arrangements for Mr. Bolt to testify, he suddenly disappeared completely, and we had no idea where he had gone — or why.'

'Then I don't see how you can expect — '

'Mr. Maddox,' Judge Craig interrupted, 'please allow me to rule on your objection before you continue.' Turning to Connie, he went on. 'Mr. Maddox has an excellent point. Do you have any deposition or other valid confirmation of this story you were told?'

'If you'll indulge us, your honor, Mr. Goldthwaite has first-hand evidence about Mr. Bolt and his whereabouts.'

'All right, proceed. But make your connection quickly.'

'Thank you, your honor. Mr. Goldthwaite, please continue.'

'Following Mr. Bolt's abrupt disappearance, my assistant and I spent several days making enquiries among the last people with whom he had contact. It seemed to us that Mr. Bolt may have been afraid his contact with us had been discovered, and that some attempt might be made to remove him from the situation.'

'What are you claiming?' Maddox was now yelling directly at Connie.

'Mr. Maddox, please take your seat, or voice your objection properly.' Judge Craig gaveled for quiet.

Maddox sat down abruptly, and Gail noticed he was making an effort now to ignore Tommy's insistent whispering. Good! Perhaps Maddox was having some second thoughts about his client's story.

'Continue.' Connie nodded to Hugo.

'Yes. Well, after questioning Mr. Bolt's acquaintances, we had a few ideas about his possible whereabouts, but nothing concrete. Then several incidents transpired that forced us to come to a decision about whether or not to pursue this line any further.'

'You say several incidents transpired,' Connie repeated. 'Please describe those incidents in as much detail as you can, bearing in mind what your personal connection or observation was in each instance.'

Hugo glanced at his notes. 'The first incident involved Ms. Brevard and her brother. This happened on July 9th, shortly after 10:00 a.m. at Seymour Park, near the mall.'

'Yes, go on.'

'Ms. Brevard had gone there with her brother on an outing. She was seated on one of the benches near the exercise ground. Her brother was making the rounds of the facility as she watched. All was well until she was suddenly accosted by Tommaso Del Monaco.'

The courtroom was eerily silent. Judge Craig stared at Hugo. 'You're saying Ms. Brevard was 'accosted' by Mr. Del Monaco? What do you mean by that?'

Maddox had started to rise but thought better of it when Craig intervened.

'I mean, your honor,' Hugo continued, 'Mr. Del Monaco approached Ms. Brevard and attempted to have a conversation with her. She explained to him that it was not permissible because of this impending trial — but he and his men refused to leave, and he continued to talk to her, making what she could only interpret as threats.'

'Preposterous!' shouted Maddox. 'I imagine my client was only attempting to pass a little harmless conversation. He perhaps didn't understand the objection she raised — '

'Mr. Maddox, I would advise you to remain seated until we hear the rest of this testimony. I'm very curious now as to the nature of this conversation. Mr. Goldthwaite,' Craig went on, turning back to Hugo, 'please continue. But I would like you to be specific about your firsthand knowledge of this supposed lapse of propriety.'

'Yes. The fact of the matter is, Ms. Brevard was concerned enough that she managed to open her phone line with me, unbeknownst to Del Monaco. As soon as I got the gist of the conversation, I recorded the rest of what he said to her. At the same time, I contacted the police and asked them to send a car to the park as quickly as possible.'

Maddox stood. 'I object, your honor. If my client was taped without his knowledge or consent — '

'Overruled,' snapped Craig.

'Continue, Mr. Goldthwaite,' said Connie.

'My assistant Jake Morrow and I got to the scene just as the police arrived. Mr. Del Monaco and two of his men were still there. He was still insisting on conversing with Ms. Brevard against her will.'

'Is there a police report?' Craig asked.

'Yes, sir,' said Connie, pulling the papers from his file. 'I have copies here for both you and Mr. Maddox. I might add, your honor, that the two men who were also present at the park are here in the courtroom today.' He gestured toward the plaintiff's table. 'They're seated two rows back of the plaintiff on the aisle.'

Craig peered out at the crowded room. 'Bailiff,' he ordered, 'I'd like you to have those two men taken aside and watched until we get through this phase of the trial.'

The two men Gail remembered from her encounter with Tommy had half-risen in their seats when they were mentioned.

A uniformed officer approached and took them to a secure location to one side. They sat there glaring, first at the defense team, then at Tommy, who tried unsuccessfully to ignore them.

Craig held up his hand for a pause while he glanced over the police report. He looked down at Tommy. 'This doesn't look very good for you,' he said, shaking his head. Then, turning back to Connie, he added, 'Proceed.'

'Yes, your honor. Mr. Goldthwaite, you said there were several incidents during that period of time. What was the next thing that happened?'

Hugo took his time. 'The next incident was of a much more serious nature. We were trying in every way possible to find Mr. Bolt. As part of that procedure, I attempted to make contact again with the informant who had brought him to our attention in the first place, but I was unsuccessful. The man, one Hector Lozano, also had disappeared. He was nowhere to be found, which was very unusual. I had all my people searching for him. But he was just gone.

'Then I received some information from one of my contacts at the city morgue. An unidentified body had been brought in under mysterious circumstances. Jake Morrow and I received permission to examine the body under the coroner's supervision. I was afraid it might be Bolt.'

'When you examined the body, were you able to make a positive I.D.?'

'No, it was impossible. The corpse had been found in the ruins of a recent fire in the warehouse district. The building had burned to the ground, and the body was fried to a crisp. Visual identification was impossible.'

'But I assume a positive identification was made eventually?'

The people at the plaintiff's table were now visibly shaken. Tommy was bent over his notepad, scribbling furiously. Maddox was pale and silent. Tommy's sister Veronica was crying, the tears streaming down her face.

'Yes. The coroner was able to get enough DNA samples to positively identify the body as that of . . . '

The entire courtroom, including Judge Craig, sat quietly in anticipation.

' . . . Hector Lozano.' Hugo sat back and awaited the next inevitable question.

'Hector Lozano, your informant?'

'Yes.'

'And was a cause of death established?'

Maddox rose wearily. 'Your honor, is all this a matter of record?'

'Your honor,' Connie said smoothly, 'I have here the death certificate signed by the coroner.' He waved a piece of paper in the direction of the bench. 'And I also have the police and fire reports that establish the cause of the fire to have been arson. There were large amounts of accelerant found in the hallway leading to the room where Lozano's body was discovered. Also, the window transom he used as an access point to the room had been nailed shut from the outside. There was no way he could have escaped the inferno. The cause of death has been ruled suspicious by the coroner's office, and the police are considering it as an ongoing investigation. I have those reports, too.'

As he pulled the appropriate paperwork from his file, the two men being watched by security made another move to get up and leave. 'Take those two men into custody,' called Judge Craig, pointing at them. 'They are not to leave until we get to the bottom of all this.'

'Your honor,' Maddox tried again, 'I still don't see what any of this has to do with today's trial. This is a civil procedure about the distribution of an estate. What, if any, relationship has it got to Nino Del Monaco's will?'

'I must have leeway to make the connection — and I will, I assure you,' Connie said to Judge Craig. 'Please, let us continue our story.'

'I agree, counselor,' Craig said. 'Mr. Maddox, you'll fare better here, I believe, if you let this tale unfold without further interruption. I for one am very curious now about all these incidents and where they may have originated, and why. Continue with your story, Mr. Goldthwaite.'

'Thank you, your honor.' Connie turned back to Hugo. 'And were there any further happenings of interest to our case?'

'Yes. All our research indicated a very good possibility that Mr. Bolt, if he had escaped intact, might have fled to Mexico. We began making enquiries along the border, concentrating on the two points of entry we thought most promising, Laredo and Brownsville.

'We got lucky in Brownsville. One of our contacts there remembered someone crossing the border a few days earlier and made a positive identification from a photo of Bolt. The subject had disguised his appearance a bit and was traveling under an assumed name, but the informant was certain it was the same man.

'Armed with the knowledge that Bolt's friend Hector Lozano had come to a bad end, we decided to try and find the man if at all possible and seek to have him deposed in Mexico City. Ms. Brevard and I immediately flew to the place Mr. Bolt had been headed — and you, Mr. Osterlitz, petitioned the Mexican National Court to arrange for the deposition to take place there, if we were unable to persuade Bolt to return here.'

'And were you successful?'

'In a manner of speaking, yes we were.'

'Explain.'

'On our first day there, through a miracle of sorts — although it was actually a matter of informed supposition — we ran into Bolt in a public place. He was surprised, of course, to see us, but was cooperative. He was as shocked as we had been at the circumstances surrounding Lozano's death. Because of that, I think, he decided to return to the United States with us. We started back that same afternoon.'

Judge Craig banged his gavel at the gasps from the spectators. 'Quiet, or I'll have the courtroom emptied,' he said. Silence ensued.

Connie continued: 'And so Mr. Bolt returned to the United States, and Cathcart, I assume, in the company of you and Ms. Brevard?'

'Yes. We put him in protective custody and were beginning to prepare him for testimony.'

'Beginning? Did something happen to interfere with that process?'

'Yes. Just as we were beginning our final preparations for this trial, we received word that Ms. Brevard's cousin, Miss Lucy Verner, disappeared from the family home in Long Hills.'

Judge Craig's voice rang out. 'Take those two men into custody,' he said, pointing at Tommy's henchmen. 'They are not to leave this courtroom *under any circumstance.*' He called the bailiff to his side and whispered further instructions. There was a brief buzz as the deputies placed handcuffs on the two men and led them to an area behind the bailiff's desk, where they sat fuming under the watchful eye of their guards.

'What happened with Miss Verner?' Craig asked, turning back to Connie.

'That incident comprises the end of our story, your honor. But I'd like Mr. Goldthwaite to continue with his narrative, with your approval.'

'Go ahead.'

Hugo paused and drank some water from the cup on the witness desk before continuing. 'Of course we were all very concerned,' he went on. 'Interestingly, Mr. Bolt had some idea of where Miss Verner might have been taken and gave us directions. I was already out in the field and headed toward the location he suggested. Jake Morrow had remained in your office that morning, and when Bolt asked to visit the men's room, Jake went with him. Bolt stumbled and nearly fell, grabbing onto Jake for support. Somehow Bolt picked Jake's pocket, took his gun and car keys, and was gone and out of the building before he was missed. You — ' He indicated Connie. ' — were able to access your office surveillance tapes and determine the direction Bolt headed. I went back to town and tried to intercept him.'

'And what happened?' Connie asked. 'Were you able to find Bolt and Miss Verner?'

'I headed to the same warehouse area where the fatal fire had taken place, thinking it was possible the events were somehow related. I spotted Jake's car pulled into a lot adjacent to a vacant warehouse near the burned facility. I called for police backup and headed in. Just as I neared the rear of the building, two shots rang out. The police were behind me as I ran toward the sound.'

'And what did you and the police discover in that room at the rear of the abandoned warehouse?'

'We found Lucy Verner.'

'And was she alive?'

'Yes, she was alive and well, considering what she'd endured. She was seated in a chair in the middle of the room, bound and gagged, but otherwise in good condition, beyond being in a state of shock.'

'And Bolt?'

'Well, that was the unfortunate part. We did find Mr. Bolt. But he had been shot in the chest at close range and was in bad shape. We did everything we could for him. Miss Verner is a retired nurse, and she rendered first aid and stayed with him until the ambulance arrived.'

'But Mr. Bolt had your assistant's gun. Was there any evidence that he had attempted to use it to protect himself?'

'Well that's just it. Apparently he wasn't aware of some of the newer innovations with the safety clips. Jake had left the safety on, and Bolt didn't know that — or didn't know how to release it. I'm sure he would have fired if he could. But he didn't have the opportunity.'

'And the assailant or assailants?'

'Got away out the back of the building. We never even caught a glimpse of them.'

'Thank you, Mr. Goldthwaite. You've been extremely helpful.' He turned to Maddox. 'Your witness,' he said, returning to his seat.

But Maddox was looking puzzled. Tommy had stopped whispering to him and Veronica sat stonily silent. The defense attorney had been blindsided with this testimony, just as Gail and Connie had hoped. Tommy had not confided all this to him as he should have. Maddox didn't have a plan of attack, so he fenced.

'Mr. Goldthwaite,' he said, glancing at the notes he had made during Hugo's testimony, 'is it your contention that these . . . these bizarre 'incidents', as you call them, have anything at all to do with Nino Del Monaco's decisions on how his estate was to be dispersed at the time of his death? If so, would you please elaborate?'

Hugo glanced at Connie, who nodded. 'I'm merely recounting a series of incidents that took place during the research I undertook at the behest of the defense team and which had the appearance of being connected.'

Maddox looked puzzled. 'But *why* did you connect them to the matter at hand? Was it suggested to you, perhaps by the defense counsel, that you *look* for connections . . . even *manufacture* them if necessary?'

Connie rose. 'Objection, your honor. Mr. Goldthwaite has merely answered the questions put to him in a factual narrative. I intend, with my next witnesses, to make the connections Mr. Maddox is seeking.'

'Be sure that you do, Mr. Osterlitz. Objection sustained. Move to another line of questioning, Mr. Maddox.'

Maddox had been gazing thoughtfully

at the two men being detained by the armed guards. He looked back at Tommy, shook his head and took his seat. 'Nothing further,' he said. 'The witness is excused, but I reserve the right to re-examine Mr. Goldthwaite later.'

'Granted. Does the defense wish to call any further witnesses?'

'Yes, your honor. We would like to call Miss Lucy Verner to the stand.'

Whispers and comments abounded. Judge Craig again gaveled for silence. All heads were turned as a sturdy older woman was ushered in who made her way down the aisle to the witness box with a sprightly step and was sworn in. Gail rose and took her place. She smiled warmly at Cousin Lucy. This would be the easiest task of the day.

'Good morning,' she said. 'Would you please state your name and occupation for the court?'

'My name is Lucy Verner. I'm a retired nurse. I'm presently residing with my cousin Alberta Norris, and her son Erle, in Long Hills.'

'Thank you. Now, I would like you to

confirm for us the circumstances described earlier by Mr. Goldthwaite.'

'Well, on the morning he spoke of, I had some items I wanted to pick up at the small grocery store near the house. I asked the security guard about it, and he suggested I wait until he could either accompany me or retrieve the things for me. I'm ashamed to say I didn't take his very good advice and insisted on going by myself. I really just wanted to get out of the house for a bit on my own.'

'Did you notice anyone following you at the time you left the house?'

'Not at first. There was a car, a black sedan, parked up near the hilltop. I know I should have been more careful, but I ignored it and went on in the other direction to the store.'

'And you entered the store, shopped, and returned to the parking lot?'

'Yes. At first I didn't notice anyone. There weren't many cars in the lot, and I'm afraid I was thinking more about my purchases and whether I had time to take a little drive before going back to the house.'

'But there was someone else there.'

'Yes. I normally park at the far end of the lot, just to force myself to walk a little bit . . . get some exercise, you know. This time was no different. But as I headed across the lot, I noticed what looked to me to be that same dark car I'd seen earlier parked near the house. It was then that I remembered what you'd said — '

'Objection!' Maddox bounded out of his chair. 'Not only is this hearsay, but the defense counsel has obviously coached this witness in exactly what to say.'

'Ms. Brevard? Counsel has a point.'

'Your honor, Ms. Verner is my cousin. We often speak together about events in our lives. But I'm prepared to have her last statement stricken completely from the record. And I can assure you that her testimony going forward will concern only the things she witnessed or heard firsthand.'

'Very well, but please be careful with your line of questioning.'

'Thank you, your honor. Now,' she said, turning back to Lucy, 'just tell us in your words exactly what happened when you approached your car in the parking lot at the Good Buy Market.'

'Well, the first thing I noticed was a man blocking my way. I didn't think anything of it, and started to go around him, when suddenly he grabbed me and forced a cloth over my mouth and nose.'

Gail waited until the courtroom hisses and whispers ceased. 'What happened next?'

'The cloth was saturated with some evil-smelling liquid — ether, or the equivalent, would be my guess. In just a few moments I lost consciousness.'

'So on the day in question, as you left the store, you were accosted, grabbed and doped into unconsciousness. Tell me, Miss Verner, did you get a good look at the man who did this terrible thing to you?'

'Yes.' A pin dropping in the courtroom would have been heard.

'Do you see that man in this courtroom now?'

'Yes, I do. *That* is the man who kidnapped me.' Lucy half-rose in her seat and pointed a finger at the smaller of the two men being held by the guards.

'Let it be noted that the witness has identified one of the prisoners being held by the court as the man who accosted and drugged her,' Gail stated.

Judge Craig glared at Tommy. The two men in question had already been connected to him by the police report. This was turning rapidly from a civil case into a criminal charge. The judge was not happy with this turn of events.

Just then the rear doors opened and the district attorney, Turner Redland, entered and took a seat quietly in one of the back rows. The bailiff had summoned him at Judge Craig's request to follow up on the men in Tommy Del Monaco's employ.

'Let me interrupt here,' Craig said. 'Bailiff, I want those two men put in handcuffs and shackles immediately. Mr. Del Monaco,' he added, looking straight at Tommy, 'you will not leave the jurisdiction of this court until this whole matter is settled, understood?'

'Yes, your honor,' Maddox responded. 'I'll vouch for Mr. Del Monaco's presence.'

'Good, see that you do. Proceed with your questions, counselor.'

'Yes, your honor.' Gail looked back at her notes. She and Turner had not always seen eye to eye on things, but in this instance she was glad for his presence.

'Miss Verner, I'm so sorry that you were subjected to such a frightening experience. But here you are today, looking fit and able to testify. Continue with your story. We need to understand — how were you able to escape from your captors?'

'When I came to a while later, I didn't have any idea where I was. Later on I discovered I'd been held in an empty warehouse on the outskirts of Cathcart. I was tied to a chair and my mouth was gagged. Those two men — ' Here she pointed at the prisoners. ' — were seated across the room from me. They didn't speak to me, but I did overhear their conversation with each other. They were saying something about how they'd get a pretty good payday out of Tommy for this job, and that they hadn't asked enough for 'burning up old Hector.' The only thing I could think was that they intended to kill me, too. I don't mind saying, I was scared to death.'

'I'm sure you must have been. So you are certain they specifically mentioned Tommy as the person who had ordered your kidnapping, as well as the burning-up of 'old Hector'?'

'Yes, I'm absolutely certain that those are the exact words they used.'

'Yet here you are, safe and unharmed. Can you explain the circumstances surrounding your escape?'

Lucy looked down. 'I owe my life to a man who was willing to give his life to save me. A man I don't even know.'

'Go on,' Gail urged. This was the most important part of Lucy's testimony.

'Just as I was about to give up hope, I saw, out of the corner of my eye, a shadow flitting across the front of the room. The men holding me were laughing and talking, not paying attention, so they didn't notice. I tried not to make any moves to distract them, but watched as the shadow became form and substance. A man suddenly appeared and took a stance to one side of me. He nodded at me to let me know he was a friend, then called out to the other two men by name.'

'What names did he call out? Do you recall?'

'Oh yes, I won't forget those names. He called out 'Manny' and 'Carl' to get their attention. He had a pistol in his hand, pointed straight at them. I was so frightened at that point that I was afraid I'd faint again, but luckily I didn't.'

'Can you describe this man, this 'friend'?'

'He was my age or older, medium height, slender build. He had black hair tied back in a short ponytail, but I think it was dyed. He had the bluest eyes I've ever seen.'

'I have an I.D. here that was used by someone to cross the border into Mexico last week. This I.D. has been matched with one belonging to one Clinton Bolt. Does this resemble the man you saw?' Gail handed it to Lucy and passed copies to the judge and Maddox.

'Yes, that's the same man. I'm sure of it.'

Tommy's head was in his hands. Maddox looked stunned.

'So the man who rescued you from your kidnappers was Clinton Bolt. Can you describe for me what happened next? How did the two men react to Bolt's demand?'

'They shot him. They pulled out their guns and shot him, that's what they did!' Lucy began to cry. 'They intended to kill him, just as they wanted to kill me. He saved my life!'

'Are you able to go on, Miss Verner?' asked Craig. 'We can take a short break, if you like.'

'No, I'm fine, your honor. I want to get this over with.'

'You say Mr. Bolt saved your life. But if your captors were in control of the situation, why didn't they kill you, too?'

'Because the police came rushing in then, after hearing the gunshots. Those two — ' She indicated the prisoners again. ' — those two bullies escaped. They ran out the back and got away. The police and Mr. Goldthwaite were busy getting me loose and trying to do what they

300

could for Mr. Bolt. I tried to give him first aid, but his injuries were so severe . . . all I could do was try to provide him some comfort until the ambulance came.' She shook her head. 'Everything was so hectic, I'm afraid I don't remember much after that.'

'Thank you, Miss Verner. You've done very well.' Gail turned to Judge Craig. 'I have no further questions, your honor.'

'Does the plaintiff's counsel wish to cross-examine?'

Maddox shook his head. 'No, your honor. No questions at this time . . . although I reserve the right to re-examine this witness further along.'

'So granted. Ms. Brevard, was this your final witness?'

'No, your honor. The defense wishes at this time to call its final witness, Clinton Bolt.'

31

When Bolt had entered the abandoned warehouse on that last day, he was not afraid. He was fairly certain what he would find there. He was incensed that Tommy had gone so far as to have an innocent woman taken and held against her will, although he wasn't surprised really. Anyone who would do the kinds of things Tommy had already done, all in the interest of hanging on to the control of that damn money . . . well, there was probably no end to the evil the man was capable of unleashing.

Bolt had checked the pistol he had lifted from Jake's pocket to make sure it was loaded. He didn't give another thought to the rest of the mechanism. He hadn't fired a gun in a very long time, but what was there to it? Point and pull the trigger. He thought he could do that much, if necessary. Beyond that, he considered the weapon a deterrent.

Maybe, if Tommy's goons got a good look at it, they would think twice about escalating the violence. He hoped his gift of persuasion would allow him to talk his way through the situation. If not, well, he would just have to cross that bridge when he got to it.

Making his way through the darkened building, he stumbled once or twice and had to catch himself to keep from making any noise. No point in giving his presence away too soon. At last he got to the back room where he determined Lucy was being held. Peeking around a pile of boxes, he saw her, caught her eye and raised a finger to his lips. She nodded slightly and looked to her right. Good. She seemed to be alert and uninjured.

He followed her line of sight and quickly spotted the two goons he knew as Manny and Carl, sitting in a couple of lawn chairs, smoking and chatting. Just a couple of good ol' boys having a good time.

He spat to relieve his dry throat, blinked his eyes rapidly to make sure his vision wasn't blurred, then stepped forward, the gun held in front of him (steadily, he hoped), and pointed straight at the two men. 'Manny! Carl!' he called out, praying his voice didn't waver.

He was about to say something else when two shots rang out. A look of surprise came over his face.

It wasn't supposed to happen this way. What had gone wrong?

★ ★ ★

'What went wrong, Mr. Bolt?' Gail had gotten him to this crucial point in his narration. 'Why didn't your gun fire?'

'I was too hesitant. I've been told since that most modern guns have what's known as a passive safety selector. You have to pull the trigger to release it. I didn't react decisively enough — probably my lack of experience. The safety didn't release as it should have, and the gun didn't fire.'

'But the two men you've identified as Manny and Carl, the men in the courtroom today, acted quickly and shot you first.'

'Yes. I lost consciousness not long afterwards. I've been told I was near death.'

'I believe that's correct. You're lucky to be able to testify today.'

Bolt nodded. He was seated in a wheelchair near the witness box. His face was pale and drawn, but he was alert and determined to testify. Before, it had been a matter of getting a big payday out of Tommy or Ralph; he didn't care which. But now it was more than that: he wanted to change his life. The only way he could do that was to face the demons of his past and move ahead into the future, free of all the lies and hiding.

Maddox rose wearily. He knew the court's sentiment was against him now, but he still had to make his best case. 'Your honor, the counsel for the plaintiff wishes at this point to acknowledge the . . . irregularities surrounding this case. But we still have the matter of Nino Del Monaco's estate to be settled. All of this is damning evidence against one of the litigants, Mr. Tommaso Del Monaco. But there are other parties to this suit who must be accounted for — namely Ms. Veronica Giuliani, who is present; and the third son, Leónardo Del Monaco, who resides in Florida and could not be here today.'

'Yes, your honor,' Gail said. 'We're getting to that. As promised, Mr. Bolt's further testimony will have a direct bearing on the outcome of this claim against the estate of Nino Del Monaco. May we continue?'

'I'm all ears, counselor,' Judge Craig said. 'No one is more curious about your further evidence than I am.'

Gail looked at Bolt with genuine concern. The next part of her questioning would be difficult for him, and she hoped that the damage he had suffered from the gunshot wounds would not prevent him from finally getting his story out in the open. 'Are you able to continue, Mr. Bolt?'

'Yes. I just want to get this over with.'

'I'll try to be as brief as possible. You recall Mr. Goldthwaite getting in touch with you to ask you about information you had concerning the Del Monaco family? He brought you to our offices to tell a story so compelling that we decided it needed to be included as a part of our preparation for this trial.'

'Yes, that's true.'

'At the time, a little over a month remained before the trial date. We decided, and you agreed, to go into semi-hiding to allow you time to rest and relax before the trial without any danger of you being compromised by the other side.'

'Yes.'

'But at some point you, thinking your own life might be in danger, left the country and went into hiding in Mexico. Can you tell us why you were afraid for your safety?'

'Sometimes you just get a feeling. I had a hunch that Tommy knew what I was up to and just might decide to do something about it. I was further convinced when I spotted a car one day that looked a lot like one I knew Tommy's men drove. I didn't hang around to make sure; I just took off.'

'But when Mr. Goldthwaite and I

found you in Mexico and informed you of the death of Hector Lozano, you changed your mind.'

'Yes. I decided if I didn't do something to change the situation, I'd end up spending the rest of my life looking over my shoulder. It wasn't worth it to me to do that. Of course, at that time I was still hoping one of them, Tommy or Ralph, would make it worth my while to skew my testimony one way or the other. But I don't care about any of that anymore. Looking death in the eye changes your priorities. Now all I want to do is see justice done.'

'Let's go back a bit, Mr. Bolt, to lay the foundation for the story you're about to tell. At one point in time, you were employed on a regular basis by the Del Monaco Hotel concern in Las Vegas and Lake Tahoe?'

'Yes. It wasn't a lot of money, but it was regular, something an old piano player like me doesn't find every day. My duties were to organize the music entertainment for both facilities, including booking shows, doing arrangements, overseeing auditions and rehearsals and the like. I did that for several years before deciding I didn't want to be tied down to a regular job like that.'

'Was there any other reason for you to decide to leave the organization?'

'Yes. Actually, it was the main reason. You see, I had a bit of a drinking problem.' He grimaced, 'It'd gotten worse, I think, as I got more bored with the situation there. I began hiding out in various spots around the buildings, to drink sometimes, and other times to recover from a drinking bout.'

'And one day when you were hiding out . . . ?'

'One day I was hiding out in one of the storerooms off of Tommy's office in the Vegas complex. I'd been sleeping on a cot when I suddenly heard voices. I got up, thinking someone might come in looking for something and discover me. That didn't happen, but I crept to the door and listened to the conversation, hoping I wouldn't get caught.'

'Were you able to distinguish the voices?'

'Yes, without a doubt. One of the speakers was Tommy. He was angry or upset about something his brother had done.'

'You mean Leónardo Del Monaco, the brother who isn't present today?'

'Yes. The third brother — Ralph's father, Carlo — had died a few years back in a private plane crash. He was on his way back here to Cathcart from Vegas, but he never made it.'

'So what were Tommaso and Leónardo discussing? And why does it have a bearing on the estate of Nino Del Monaco?'

'Tommy was trying to talk Lennie — Leónardo — into doing something illegal. Something big, having to do with an association with one of the Columbian drug cartels. Lennie didn't want to do it. He said — and I'm quoting as close as I can here — he said, 'You tried to get Carlo to do the same thing and he refused. Are you going to kill me now, too?' Believe me, when I heard that, I thought I was going to give myself away right then and there. I tried to stay as

310

quiet as I could, and hoped I wouldn't get caught. I knew if Tommy found me there, I'd be a goner.'

The courtroom was utterly still. Judge Craig's attention was riveted on the pale face of Clinton Bolt. Ralph Del Monaco was staring with undisguised hatred at his uncle Tommy. His aunt Veronica had sunk forward and was sobbing silently, her chest heaving with each gasp.

Gail allowed the silence to continue a moment longer as she perused her notes. Finally, she looked up and continued. 'And then what happened? Did the argument between Tommy and Lennie end peacefully?'

'No, it did not.' He straightened up as much as his condition allowed. 'Through that crack in the door, I saw Tommy shoot Lennie through the forehead. I saw that, and I saw Lennie fall to the floor, stone-cold dead. Then Tommy called in Manny and Carl and told them to 'clean up this mess.' I hid in a storage cabinet for a long time, until no more sounds came from the office. I got out of there, went back to my room at the hotel, packed my things, cashed in my chips and left town, pretty much in that order. I haven't been back to Vegas since.'

'Did Tommy try to find you, to question you as to why you left?'

'No. Never occurred to him. I was a boozy piano player, nobody he was concerned about. I sent my notice to the casino manager. I doubt anyone was surprised. In that business, people come and go all the time. I spent the next few years traveling around from gig to gig. I finally ended up back here in Cathcart. I figured by now all that would've died down. If nobody had found out I was in that room by now, I thought I was clear.'

'So why did you volunteer to testify in this case?'

'When I heard Nino had died, and that the family, headed by Tommy, was trying to sue Ralph for the estate, it kind of made me mad. Also, I thought I might be able to make some sort of a payday out of what I knew.'

'A payday?'

'Yes. I thought my information was

worth something to someone. My preference was Ralph. Knowing what I knew about his father's death, I thought he probably deserved the estate. I knew damn well Tommy didn't.'

'So how do you think Tommy got wind you were going to testify?'

'It was planned. Poorly, I'll admit, but I did have something in mind. I think now that Hector Lozano must've said the wrong thing to someone about it. I trusted him, and under ordinary circumstances I don't think he would've let anything slip. But I think he maybe had too much to drink one night and bragged a bit. I'd promised him a cut of whatever I might get out of it. I think he let the cat out of the bag.'

'But you realize you can't be paid for testifying?'

'Yes, but there are *expenses*, you see. Just like an expert witness might get paid for his time and expenses, I thought I might get reimbursed the same way. Anyway, after poor old Hector bought the farm, I wanted to do it just to settle the score. That was a terrible way for that man to die. But now I don't care anymore. I just want to see that man locked away where he can't hurt anyone again.'

Clinton Bolt stared long and hard at Tommaso Del Monaco, who could not meet his eyes. Then he sighed. 'I'm pretty tired, Ms. Brevard. I think I need to rest now.'

32

The trial was over. It had not taken Judge Craig long to come to a decision about the division of Nino Del Monaco's estate.

He ruled that Veronica Giuliani and her children, and the son and daughter of the deceased Leónardo Del Monaco, were all entitled to a pro rata portion of the monetary assets. Tommaso Del Monaco, who had no children, was barred from realizing anything at all from his father's estate. He and his cohorts, Manny and Carl, were remanded back to criminal court to stand trial for their transgressions. D.A. Redland would have his headline-making case to cement his re-election campaign, and Tommy Del Monaco would be lucky if he ever saw the light of day again. The miscellaneous businesses and real property holdings that made up the bulk of Nino's fortune all went to Ralph, who was more than satisfied with these arrangements. He spoke with his aunt and arranged to meet with her and his cousins at a later date to iron out the details of the settlement. The firm of Osterlitz and Brevard was rewarded with a substantial set of fees based on a percentage of the assets of the estate, together with all their court and out-of-pocket costs.

'I guess it paid off for Hugo and me to take that trip to Mexico after all,' Gail said. 'All we have to do now is figure out how to pay the taxes on our windfall.'

'It paid off, all right — but if you ever decide to do something like that again, you'd better be sure I'm going with you,' Connie said.

'Well, why don't we take a trip later on, once all this settles down? I'd love to show you San Miguel. It looked like a great place for a vacation.'

'You wouldn't mind going back there?'

'Not if it was for pleasure this time.'

'Hmm. Let's add it to the agenda. I have a feeling we'll both be ready for some down time once we get the Del Monaco affair settled for good.'

* ★ *

A few months later, just as the late-morning sun peeked over the colonial-style buildings in the background and bounced off the cobblestone street, an older man hesitated just outside a cantina near the plaza. His hair was gray and short; a buzz cut, almost. He was dressed in a neat dark suit and carried a bouquet of roses in his hand. His eyes were a brilliant and penetrating blue.

Angus Shepherd, thanks to the generosity of Ralph Del Monaco, had made the last payment on the money he had owed to Dante's employer in Mexico City. He had caught up the outstanding utility bills associated with his little *casita*, and he had also established an annuity for Luci and Miguel that would provide them with a living far into the future.

The rest of his big payoff he had deposited at the local bank again. It was more than enough to last well into his old age. And with his loan paid off and Tommy and his gang safely put away in prison, he felt safe, for the first time in a very long time.

The lock clicked and the door to the little eatery opened to the day. '*Hola*,' said *Mozo*, spotting Angus. 'Come on in. What can I get you?'

'*Hola*,' said the man who had been Bolt. '*¿Dónde está Lila?* Where is she?'

'She's in the kitchen, getting the coffee ready. Go on back.'

'*Gracias*.'

Angus Shepherd — he who had been Clinton Bolt — entered the cantina with an intense sense of anticipation.

But hopefully there would be no more change-ups any time soon.

Looked like just another tequila sunrise in his future.

We do hope that you have enjoyed reading this large print book.

Did you know that all of our titles are available for purchase?

We publish a wide range of high quality large print books including:
**Romances, Mysteries, Classics
General Fiction
Non Fiction and Westerns**

Special interest titles available in large print are:
**The Little Oxford Dictionary
Music Book, Song Book
Hymn Book, Service Book**

Also available from us courtesy of Oxford University Press:
**Young Readers' Dictionary
(large print edition)
Young Readers' Thesaurus
(large print edition)**

For further information or a free brochure, please contact us at:
**Ulverscroft Large Print Books Ltd.,
The Green, Bradgate Road, Anstey,
Leicester, LE7 7FU, England.
Tel:** (00 44) **0116 236 4325
Fax:** (00 44) **0116 234 0205**

Other titles in the
Linford Mystery Library:

THIS IS THE HOUSE

Shelley Smith

On a picturesque West Indies island, the capital is dominated by the house on the mountaintop: the house that Jacques built. Premier Justice Antoine Jacques was divinely happy with his beautiful wife Julia and their son Raoul — until Julia was stricken with total paralysis . . . For years now, La Morte, as she is known, has been confined to her bed. Then, one day, she is found dead. And Quentin Seal, author of detective stories, is begged by Antoine to investigate . . .

THE SNARK WAS A BOOJUM

Gerald Verner and Chris Verner

When William Baker is found dead, his naked and twisted body lying under a bench in the dingy waiting room of a train station, the village police are baffled. Soon afterward another corpse appears, this time posthumously stuffed into full evening dress, with black pigment smeared on his face. A murderer is at large whose M.O. is to use his victims to recreate scenes from Lewis Carroll's nonsense poem, 'The Hunting of the Snark' — and it's up to amateur detective Simon Gale to stop him before he kills again.

JUNGLE QUEST

Denis Hughes

For several months, the British and European security agencies in Africa have been intercepting coded secret radio messages that are being received and responded to by a radio station hidden in the almost impenetrable depths of the Congo jungle. It's clear that some dastardly international plot is afoot. A top agent is despatched to investigate, but his reports cease abruptly, and weeks pass without further communication from him. So renowned jungle explorer Rex Brandon is hired to head an expedition to locate and neutralise the danger . . .